SHERLOCK JONES

THE PHANTOM AIRPLANE

SHERLOCK JONES

THE PHANTOM AIRPLANE

ED DUNLOP

JOURNEY FORTH™

Greenville, South Carolina

Library of Congress Cataloging-in-Publication Data

Dunlop, Ed, 1955-

Sherlock Jones : the phantom airplane / by Ed Dunlop.

p. cm.

Summary: Penny and Sherlock and two of their Christian friends spend a week at a cabin on Thunderbird Lake, where they try to solve a dangerous mystery involving the secretive flights of an airplane.

ISBN 1-59166-333-4 (perfect bound pbk. : alk. paper)

[1. Christian life—Fiction. 2. Mystery and detective stories.] I. Title: Phantom airplane. II. Title.

PZ7.D92135Sgm 2005

[Fic]—dc22

2005004556

Design by Craig Oesterling

Cover illustration by Marie Tabler

Composition by Melissa Matos

© 2005 BJU Press

Greenville, SC 29614

Printed in the United States of America

ISBN 1-59166-333-4

15 14 13 12 11 10 9 8 7 6 5 4 3 2 1

To the precious kids and dedicated workers
at Gospel Light Baptist Church
in Walkertown, North Carolina.
Molly Beeson,
Richard and JoAnne Gerber,
Jerry and JoAnne Misere,
you have been a blessing
and encouragement to me.

*"For where your treasure is,
there will your heart be also."*
Matthew 6:21

CONTENTS

ONE

ASBESTOS HAZARD

It all started on a really weird Monday morning. I knew as soon as I woke up that something was wrong, but I wasn't sure just what it was. I lay still for a moment, trying hard to figure out what was amiss. Something was wrong. I could feel it. But I just couldn't put my finger on it. I just had this uneasy feeling that something bad was about to happen.

I finally rolled over in bed and looked at the clock. Oh, no! The display was flashing 12:00 in bright red numerals. The power had gone off sometime during the night!

I sat up in bed and grabbed my watch off the nightstand. 7:18. My alarm hadn't gone off. I had only twelve minutes to get to the bus stop! I should have been up forty-eight minutes ago!

Leaping out of bed, I pulled my nightgown over my head as I ran to the closet.

I seized my peach-colored blouse and threw it on. There wasn't time to button it now; I could do that on the way down the stairs. I jumped into a skirt without even noticing what color it was.

My watch said 7:20 as my trembling fingers attempted to fasten the strap around my wrist. Why is it so hard to move fast when you really need to? I thrust my feet into a pair of sneakers. The laces would have to wait until I got the toaster started.

Dashing down the hall to the bathroom, I splashed some water on my face and ran a brush through my thin blond hair. As usual, my hair refused to cooperate. I pumped about half a bottle of hair spray onto my hair and then dropped the bottle in the sink. There wasn't time to do more. I made a face at the reflection in the mirror. How I hated that unmanageable blond hair, and how I despised those freckles!

I remembered to button my blouse as I ran down the stairs. Raising one elbow, I checked my watch. 7:22. If I hurried, I'd have just enough time to toast an English muffin, smear it with apple butter, and eat it as I ran for the bus stop. I just hoped that Mom had my lunch made.

"My alarm clock didn't go off!" I wailed as I dashed into the kitchen where Mom and Dad sat at the breakfast table. "I think the power was out during the night! I'm gonna be late for sure!"

Dad lowered his newspaper to glance over at the battery-powered clock by the sink. "Slow down, Penny," he said calmly. "You'll make it."

I grabbed an English muffin from the counter and struggled to separate it into two halves. "I'm gonna miss the bus!"

Mom took a juice glass from the cabinet. She stepped over beside me and poured me a glass of orange juice. "Your father's right, Penny," she said. "Calm down. I know you're running late, but you'll make it."

I plunked the English muffin halves into the toaster and pushed the lever down. Then I took a deep breath. "OK," I sighed, "I'm calm." I grabbed a small plate from the cabinet and reached for the refrigerator door.

Jerking the refrigerator door open, I snatched the apple butter off the shelf. And that's when it happened. Disaster! A gallon jug of milk came leaping out at me. I saw the jug of milk falling, but I had the plate in one hand and the apple butter in the other. So I tried to swing the door closed with my elbow. Another wrong move. The door started to close, struck the falling jug of milk, and bounced open again. I guess the impact was what caused an aerosol can of whipped cream to fall out of the rack in the door.

The jug of milk landed on its side on the floor. Unfortunately, the plastic jug wasn't the type with the screw-on cap; it was one of those snap-on jobs that never stay on right. The top popped off, and the milk began to pour from the jug with a funny *glug-glug* sound.

But that wasn't as bad as the can of whipped cream. I still believe that aerosol cans are for deodorant and hair spray, not whipped cream. When the can fell from the refrigerator door, it landed squarely on that white plastic nozzle those cans always have. The impact bent the nozzle at a strange angle and somehow triggered the release valve inside the can. A pressurized stream of whipped cream sprayed from the can.

The can went rolling across the kitchen floor, spraying whipped cream the whole time. One moment the nozzle was pointing up in the air, splattering a fountain of whipped cream across the room; the next moment, the nozzle was spraying the floor, then up in the air again. It was a regular blizzard! The jug of milk still lay on its side in an ever-growing pool of wasted milk.

I stared at the mess for just a fraction of a second, and then my brain clicked into gear. I grabbed for the milk jug. No sense in waiting for the entire gallon to pour out.

I suppose that I forgot that I had the jar of apple butter in my hand. When I reached for the milk jug, I saw a blur of motion out of the corner of my eye as the apple butter went sailing in a shallow arc to land in the middle of the kitchen floor. The jar didn't break, but—you guessed it—the lid came off. Apple butter splattered everywhere.

I reached for the jar, stepped in the apple butter, and lost my footing. I landed smack in a puddle of milk and apple butter.

Mom to the rescue! She stooped and seized the milk jug, which was still busily dispensing free milk. Dad dropped his paper and dived for the errant can of whipped cream, which was still rolling and distributing whipped cream.

He tried. He really did. But he forgot that the floor was covered in milk and apple butter. When he hit that mess, his feet flew out from under him. He slid across the floor on his stomach and crashed into Mom's knees, causing her to drop the jug of milk and fall on top of him.

I reached over and picked up the milk jug, which by this time was nearly empty. I set it upright on the floor and then glanced in the direction that the can of whipped cream had taken. Fortunately, by now the can had reached the wall and stopped rolling. The can gave one last hiss, shot a final blob of whipped cream up on the wall, and then grew quiet. At last, it was empty. The contents covered the kitchen—ceiling, walls, and floor. It looked as if someone had planted a bomb inside a wedding cake and then detonated it inside our kitchen.

"Oh, Penny," Mom moaned. "Just look at this place!"

"Look at my clothes!" I wailed. "They look like I got into a milk and apple butter fight. I'll never make the bus in time!"

"Well, take a look at my suit," Dad replied. "I can't go to work like this."

"You two run upstairs and change," Mom said slowly. "I'll clean up the kitchen."

"But I'm gonna miss my bus," I protested.

"I think Dad will drop you off at school on his way to work," Mom replied as she picked up the apple butter jar. "Hurry up and change your clothes. I'll have your muffins waiting for you, but I'm afraid we're out of apple butter."

I dashed into my room and started unbuttoning my blouse. Milk was still dripping from the hem of my skirt. Just then, my walkie-talkie began to beep insistently. I snatched it up angrily. "Sherlock, I can't talk right now!" I blurted, squeezing the talk button on the unit. "I'm already late! The bus is coming in about three minutes!"

"Penny, wait," Sherlock's voice responded. "You have all the time in the world. There's no school today. Over."

"What are you talking about?" I snarled. "It's Monday, isn't it? Over."

"We get an unexpected vacation," Sherlock replied. "I just heard it on the radio. Over."

My friend Sherlock was not the type of guy who clowns around a lot, but this was only the fifth week of school. I knew that the school board wasn't about to give us extra time off. "Sherlock, is this some kind of a dumb joke? If it is, it's not funny! I'm running late. Over."

"It's not a joke, Penny," came Sherlock's patient voice. "We have the week off. They found asbestos in one of the classrooms. Over."

"Asbestos?" I echoed. I don't know if I even remembered to push the talk button, so Sherlock may not have even heard me.

"Asbestos was used as a fire retardant insulation in the walls and ceilings of public buildings," Sherlock explained, "until someone decided that it might pose a slight cancer risk. Several years ago they removed it from all the buildings at Spencerville Junior High. It was an extremely costly project—several hundred thousand dollars, I believe. Anyway, they missed the ceiling in Room 301. Over."

"The band room?" I exclaimed. "Over."

"Right," Sherlock replied. "The janitor found it Saturday and reported it to the school board. They called an emergency meeting and decided that school can't reopen until Room 301 is asbestos-free. I just heard it on the news five minutes ago. Over."

"Why don't they just close down the band room until the asbestos is removed?" I asked. "Wouldn't that be simpler? Over."

I heard Sherlock sigh. "Sure it would be simpler, but do bureaucrats ever look for the simplest solution? They're estimating that it will cost more than eighty thousand dollars just to do that one room. They're insisting on shutting down the whole school while they do it, so we'll be out of school for about a week. Over."

"So you're sure that we don't have to go in this morning?" I asked, trying to verify what I was hearing. It was too good to be true. "Over."

"Right," Sherlock responded. "They're running the buses this morning to pick up the kids who didn't hear the announcement, but all they're going to do is have an assembly to announce the closing and then send everyone back home. Over."

"Hey, thanks for telling me!" I told Sherlock enthusiastically. "This just might turn out to be a good day after all. Over."

"I just thought I'd save you a trip to the bus stop," he replied. "Maybe we can do something together this afternoon."

"I'm open," I told him. "Hey, I've got to get a shower. Thanks again for telling me. Over and out."

"You're welcome, Penny. Over and out."

I switched the unit off and dropped it on the bed. Then I punched one fist into the air to show my appreciation for the unexpected reprieve from school. "Yes!"

Little did I know that within hours Sherlock and I would be hundreds of miles from home. We would soon be facing one of the most unusual and dangerous situations you could ever imagine.

TWO

THUNDERBIRD LAKE

I suppose that by now you've figured out that I don't handle emergencies very well. My name is Penny Gordon, and I'm a seventh-grader at Spencerville Junior High. My parents and I live in the little town of Willoughby, which is hardly more than a dot on the map. Our town is so small that the city fathers made the speed limit twenty-five just so that it will take you at least a full minute to drive through town. We don't even have a junior high school, so I have to take the bus to Spencerville.

I'm tall and thin, with blond hair and more freckles than you could count in half an hour. I make mostly Bs in school, but I have to work pretty hard to do that. I was saved when I was seven, and my parents and I go to Calvary Baptist Church, which just happens to be the only Bible-preaching church in Willoughby. There isn't much more to tell you about myself.

Sherlock Jones, the voice on the walkie-talkie, is one of my best friends, even if he is a boy. He's a brain—straight As, without even trying. It's not really fair.

Sherlock's real name is Jasper, but no one ever calls him that. On several occasions he's proved himself to be a real detective, even solving cases that had the police baffled, and everyone in town calls him Sherlock. I really think he's as smart as Einstein was. Maybe smarter because he at least knows how to comb his hair. Einstein didn't. Ever see his picture?

Sherlock is a year younger than the other kids in our homeroom because he skipped third grade. He's a skinny little guy with thick glasses. The first time you meet him you'd think he was a fourth- or fifth-grader. He's that little. But he's smarter than a lot of adults, and he's an absolute genius on a computer. He's also one of those rare people who can read an entire book and then recite it word for word. It's called a photographic memory.

Like me, Sherlock is an only child, and he and his parents are saved. They go to the same church we do. Sherlock is a real Christian and wants to do what's right, and he's not afraid to speak up for the Lord when the situation calls for it. He's fun to be around, but his detective work has gotten us into real trouble once or twice.

I ran downstairs and told Mom about the break from school and then headed back upstairs. I took a quick shower and changed clothes. As I started toward the hallway with my messy clothes, the walkie-talkie began to beep. I grabbed it up. "Penny here. Over."

"Penny," Sherlock's voice asked, "can you ride with me over to the Diamonds'? Lisa just called and asked us to come over. She seemed really excited about something, but she wouldn't tell me about it on the phone. Over."

"I think I can," I replied, squeezing the talk button. "Let me check with Mom. Hang on a minute. Over."

I dropped the walkie-talkie on the bed, snatched up my milk and apple butter-saturated clothing, and dashed downstairs. I hurried through the kitchen, surprised to see that the whipped cream explosion was already cleaned up. Mom was in the laundry room, so I dumped the clothes at her feet. "Can I—may I ride over to Lisa's with Sherlock? He thinks something's up, but Lisa won't tell him about it. May I?"

My pretty, curly-haired mom frowned for a moment, and then said sternly, "Young lady, after making such a mess this morning, I don't think you're going anywhere for a long, long time!"

My heart sank. "It was an accident, Mom. I didn't mean to."

"Penny, do you realize how much extra work you made for me with your little *accident*? Not to mention the wasted milk, whipped cream, and apple butter!"

I hung my head. "I'm sorry I'm such a klutz."

Mom grinned suddenly. "I'm teasing you, honey. Be home by noon."

"Thanks, Mom!" I shouted as I dashed for the stairs. Ten minutes later, Sherlock and I were pedaling for the Diamonds' house.

Lisa lives in a huge house at the north edge of town while Sherlock and I both live on the west end. Lisa's dad is the principal owner and CEO of Diamond Computer Technology, a highly successful company. He's worth millions. Just about two weeks ago, two men kidnapped Lisa, waiting until her father got two-point-four million dollars in ransom money. Sherlock saved Lisa's life by helping the police and the FBI figure out where she was.

Lisa is in our homeroom at school. She's probably the most beautiful person I've ever known, both in appearance and personality. She's tall and slender, with long, dark hair and a beautiful smile. Lisa loves the Lord with all her heart, and she's always cheerful and happy. She's a real encouragement to me to live for the Lord. You'd never guess from being around her that she's a rich kid; she's just an ordinary person like me.

"So do you have any idea what Lisa wanted?" I asked, pedaling furiously to catch up with Sherlock. Sherlock always rides fast.

"She wouldn't say," he answered, "but I detected a note of excitement in her voice. It was as if she had some big surprise to spring on us."

My curiosity was getting the best of me. "Let's hurry!" I shouted, pedaling hard and pulling ahead of him. Five minutes later we were rolling into the circular driveway of the Diamond mansion. I say mansion because really that's what it is. Lisa's house has three stories with decks on each level. It's as big as a hotel, and they have a huge pool in the backyard that's shaped just like a giant guitar.

Lisa was waiting for us. She was sitting on the front steps with her arm around one of the marble lions when we braked to a stop. She stood as Sherlock and I bounded up the stairs. "So what's the big secret?" Sherlock asked.

Lisa looked puzzled. "Secret?" she echoed. "I didn't say anything about a secret."

"No," Sherlock admitted, "but I could tell by your voice that you had something to tell us. What's up?"

Lisa blushed. "You can't read people's minds, can you?"

Sherlock laughed. "Not over the phone anyway," he replied. "Now, tell us—what's up?"

Lisa smiled that beautiful smile of hers. "How would you two like to spend the next few days at Thunderbird Lake?"

"Thunderbird Lake?" I echoed. "Where's that?"

"It's several hundred miles north of here, less than a hundred miles from the Canadian border," Lisa replied. "The lake is very secluded, and few people even know where it is. Daddy has a nice cabin there. It's beautiful in October with all the leaves changing."

"Sounds good," Sherlock replied. "How about a few details?"

"Well, Daddy has a powerful speed boat, and two wave runners, and—"

"It all sounds good," Sherlock said patiently, "but how about a few details of the trip? When would we go? Who would go with us? When would we get back? Just the facts, ma'am, just the facts."

"Oh." Lisa brushed a lock of that beautiful black hair back from her face. "Daddy was planning to drive up today and spend the next few days working on some plans for Diamond Computer. He likes to go up to the cabin and pray when he has some big decisions coming up. Anyway, when he heard that we had this week off from school, he thought that he'd take me along, and that you two might want to come too. Mom is staying home with my brothers and sisters. Oh, by the way, we need to leave about eleven."

"That doesn't give us much time to pack," I commented.

Lisa shrugged. "Just throw some old clothes in a suitcase," she replied. "We'll probably be doing some hiking, so bring your sneakers."

Sherlock got a faraway look in his eyes, and I noticed it. I elbowed him gently. "Whatcha thinking about?"

"This sounds like a lot of fun," he said soberly. "Wouldn't it be great if Brandon could go?"

The front door opened just then, and Mr. Diamond stepped out on the porch. He's a tall, slim man with broad shoulders and curly blond hair. He never dresses like a millionaire; he usually wears jeans and boots and a western shirt. You'd think he was a cowboy instead of a rich CEO. "Hi ya, Sherlock and Penny," he greeted us. "Goin' with us to the cabin?"

"We're all for it, if our parents let us go," Sherlock answered.

Lisa stepped forward and put an arm around her father's waist. "Daddy, Sherlock wants to know if Brandon Marshall can come with us. Could he? He's a new Christian, and he doesn't have much chance to be around other Christians, and . . ."

Mr. Diamond laughed. "OK, sweetheart, you don't have to sell me on the idea. Brandon can go. That will give Sherlock someone to talk to while you girls are talking girl talk." He opened the front door and gestured to Sherlock and me. "Why don't you come in and call your folks?"

I was so excited that my hands were shaking as I dialed our number. Mom answered on the third ring. "Mom, can I go, can I go? I think Sherlock's going, and Lisa's going, and Mr. Diamond, and maybe even Brandon! It's gonna be fun! Can I go, Mom? Can I? *Please,* say yes!"

"Whoa, Penny, whoa," Mom said. "Slow down a bit, girl. What's this all about?"

I took a deep breath. "Mr. Diamond is taking Lisa up to their cabin on Thunderbird Lake all this week, and they've invited Sherlock and me to go along, and we're supposed to leave about eleven. May I go, Mom? Please say yes!"

"Eleven this morning? That doesn't give us much time. I'll have to call your father at work."

"Please tell him to say yes."

Mom laughed. "Why don't you ride home and start getting ready, sweetheart. I'll check with your father while you're coming home."

"Thanks, Mom! See ya!" I hung up the phone. "I think I can go!"

Sherlock was hanging up another phone at the same time. "I'm in! Now let's call Brandon."

Lisa handed him a phone book. "Here. You can look up Brandon's number."

Sherlock grinned. "Thanks, but I'll use my own directory." He closed his eyes. "Manson . . . Marshall . . . here it is! Wanda Marshall. 698-4397." He opened his eyes.

Lisa stared at him. "You had his number memorized?"

A sudden thought occurred to me and I turned to Sherlock. "Do you have the entire Willoughby phone book memorized? Tell me the truth." Sometimes he's a little bashful about his incredible mental abilities.

Sherlock shrugged. "It's just over six hundred listings. I got bored in study hall one day."

I just shook my head, but Lisa stared open-mouthed at Sherlock. "Incredible!" she breathed.

It was almost eleven o'clock when I heard Mr. Diamond pull into our gravel driveway. "He's here, Mom!" I squealed. "Gotta go!"

Mom grabbed me in a fierce hug. "Have a good time, and mind your manners. Call us Wednesday night after church."

I grabbed my suitcase and ran outside. Mr. Diamond was driving one of those really neat custom vans, and was it fancy! I opened the door and saw a plush, plush interior—captain's chairs, TV, DVD player, individual stereo and air conditioner controls, the works! It was one nice van! I climbed into the captain's chair by the door, dragging my suitcase after me. Sherlock was in the back. He took my suitcase and stuck it behind the seat.

"Glad you could come, Penny," Mr. Diamond said. "Sherlock, show me how to get to Brandon's."

I turned to Lisa. "Is he coming?" She nodded happily.

Brandon was waiting for us at the end of his driveway probably because he didn't want Lisa and Mr. Diamond to see the shack in which he and his mom lived. I stepped out of the van so that he could go back with Sherlock. As Brandon climbed into the van, I was surprised to see that he had his clothes in a paper sack, one of those big brown ones that you get at the grocery store. "Hi, everybody," he said hesitantly.

Brandon used to be a really rough character. He failed twice in school, so he's two years older than most of the kids in our grade. He's nearly six feet tall now, with a muscular build. He has a crew cut and wears an earring in one ear. His mom is an alcoholic, and he doesn't have a dad. Brandon used to be the leader of a gang of toughs in our town, but Lisa gave him a gospel tract and witnessed to him, and he got saved. I've been amazed at the change in him. Brandon Marshall, the tough guy who used to cuss and do drugs and beat up on people, is now trying to live for the Lord.

I stared at Brandon. "Your earring is gone," I observed. "What happened?"

Brandon seemed embarrassed. "I took it out," he said, ducking his head. "I noticed that none of the Christian men at church wear them, but the druggies and rock stars do. I just didn't want to be identified with people who are against the Lord."

Lisa smiled at him. "I'm proud of you, Brandon, for making that decision."

He nodded, still embarrassed. "I'm serious about living for God," he said softly. I stared at him. What a difference salvation makes in a person!

Mr. Diamond looked at his watch as the van accelerated onto the highway. "Eleven-twenty," he said in a pleased voice. "We should make Thunderbird Lake before dark."

"Weren't you going to pick up some CDs for the computer, Daddy?" Lisa prompted.

"Thanks, sweetheart. I guess we can get them when we pass through Idaville."

Half an hour later we stopped at a big office supply store. "I'll just be a minute," Mr. Diamond said as he swung the van into a parking space.

"Do you mind if I come in, sir?" Sherlock asked. "I always like to check out the computers."

The tall man grinned. "Sure, you can all come. But you'll only have sixty seconds to look at computers." We followed him into the store.

A clerk met us halfway down the computer aisle. "Help you, sir?"

"I just need some recordable CDs," Mr. Diamond told him.

"We carry two brands," the clerk replied, "DataTech and MegaMaster, and they're both on special this week. You get one free CD with a ten-pack of either brand, so really, you're getting eleven. The quality should be basically be the same with either. DataTech is about seventy cents more for the ten-pack, but you get a lifetime guarantee."

Sherlock picked up a package of DataTech CDs and quickly scanned the information on the back. "The lifetime guarantee is worthless," he announced.

The clerk looked just a bit annoyed. "DataTech is a reputable company," he replied, giving Sherlock a stern look.

Sherlock shrugged. "I'm sure they are, but their guarantee is worthless."

The clerk sighed. "How can you say that?"

Sherlock read aloud from the package. "Lifetime warranty. In the event of the failure of any DataTech compact disk to perform satisfactorily, simply return the defective disk to DataTech along with fifty cents to cover handling costs."

The clerk smiled. "See? What more could you ask for?"

Sherlock frowned. "You could offer a lifetime warranty on any product with terms like that," he replied. "No thinking customer would ever cash in on it."

The clerk frowned. "And why not?"

"Because it would cost fifty-five cents postage, plus the fifty cent handling fee, plus the cost of the envelope or mailer," Sherlock explained. "Look at what the CDs cost to begin with! Eleven for $6.99—let's see, that's sixty-three point fifty-four cents each. Why would anyone pay a dollar five plus the cost of the mailer to replace a CD that costs less than sixty-four cents originally?"

The clerk seemed stunned as Sherlock did the calculation in his head with lightning speed. I think he realized that Sherlock's logic made sense. He shook his head, shrugged, and walked away. Mr. Diamond laughed. "We'll buy MegaMaster," he said.

After Mr. Diamond paid for the CDs, Lisa handed a gospel tract to the cashier. "Would you please read this when you get the chance?" she asked sweetly.

The cashier glanced at the tract. "Sure will," he answered pleasantly. "Thanks, young lady."

As we walked to the van I thought about what Lisa had done. Even though I'm young, I try to be faithful to read my Bible and pray and maintain a walk with the Lord. I want to serve God when I grow up. But Lisa is my age, and she's already witnessing and passing out tracts. It's as if she's not going to wait until she's grown; she wants God to use her now. It's something to think about.

A short while later we were zipping down the freeway. The van was comfortable! We talked and joked as we sped along. Brandon seemed to enjoy being with us.

Mr. Diamond glanced in his rearview mirror. "The guy coming up behind me must be doing ninety," he said. "He's really moving!"

We all turned around. A black BMW about a quarter mile back was closing in on us rapidly.

Sherlock grinned and dug into his backpack. "I'll slow him down," he promised.

I laughed at him. "How are you going to do that?"

He just smiled. "Watch and see."

The BMW flashed past us with a roar of exhaust. I glanced back at Sherlock and saw that he was holding a small plastic box a little smaller than a VCR tape. The box had a push button on top, so I figured it must be some sort of electronic gadget.

"What does that do?" I asked. Sherlock's device had also caught the attention of Lisa and Brandon, and they both leaned closer.

Sherlock pushed the button. "Watch the BMW," he instructed. We all spun around to look at the speeding car, and to our amazement, saw the red glow of brake lights! The driver of the black BMW was braking hard! He slowed down until his speed matched ours and then dropped in behind us.

Lisa looked at Sherlock in amazement. "What did you do?" she gasped. "He slowed down, just like you said he would!"

Sherlock grinned. "Anyone running that fast is probably using a radar detector," he answered, "so I just activated his detector. He slowed down to avoid getting a ticket."

I frowned. "You activated his radar detector? How?"

"With a pulse of radar," Sherlock answered.

Brandon stared at the box in my friend's hands. "That's a radar gun? How fast was he going?"

Sherlock shook his head. "It's not a gun, and it doesn't register a vehicle's speed; it simply sends a pulse of radar, which activates the detector. I just built it to have some fun with the other motorists."

Moments later the BMW swung back into the left lane and accelerated hard. Sherlock grinned and handed the plastic box to me. "Slow him down, Penny."

I pushed the button, and just like before the car slowed down. We could see that the driver was getting steamed. He was scanning his rearview mirror, hitting the steering wheel in frustration, and talking to himself. I laughed as he fell in behind us again. "This is great!"

Sherlock smiled. "I thought it might break up the monotony of the trip," he replied.

We each took turns with Sherlock's device. We slowed the BMW down three more times and then let him go by leaving the button alone for several minutes. We turned our attention to other motorists who were speeding, and there were plenty. It was great fun!

A blond woman driving a sleek red Corvette flew past us so fast, we figured she must have been doing a hundred. When Brandon pushed the button on Sherlock's "speeder spooker," the woman braked so hard that smoke poured from her tires, and the car fishtailed slightly from side to side. She dropped her speed down to sixty-five for two or three miles and then took off again.

Another push of the button, and she was back to sixty-five. We were laughing so hard that tears ran down our faces. Brandon handed the device to Sherlock. "Here," he snickered, "it's your turn!" He wiped tears from his eyes. "I've never had so much fun in all my life!"

The Corvette stayed a hundred yards ahead of us for about three more miles, and then with a puff of smoke from the exhaust pipes sped ahead. Sherlock pushed the button several times, but it had no effect. Within a minute, the Corvette was out of sight. Sherlock chuckled. "She must be in a awful hurry," he remarked, "or she figures that her radar detector is on the blink. She must be doing a hundred and ten." He slipped the device back into his backpack. "Well, enough of that for a while." He took out a book, *Advanced Theories of Quantum Physics*, and began to read.

Two or three minutes later, as the van topped a rise in the road, Mr. Diamond started to laugh. "Look," he said, pointing. "I think you set her up!"

A state trooper's car with blue lights flashing sat at the side of the freeway. Parked in front of the patrol car was a red Corvette. A trooper in a gray uniform was standing beside the driver's door, writing the woman a ticket!

"That's not fair," I said to Sherlock. "You did set her up. She ignored her radar detector when it went off for real, and she walked right into a ticket."

Sherlock shrugged. "She was speeding, wasn't she? She deserved a ticket. When she pulled away from us she must have been doing over a hundred."

Mr. Diamond laughed. "Sherlock's right," he said to me. "The driver of the Corvette was breaking the law, and now she's getting the ticket she deserves." He glanced at Sherlock and shook his head. "But how about keeping that little device away, pal, rather than getting any more drivers into trouble?"

Late that afternoon, Mr. Diamond pulled off the freeway and began to follow a narrow, winding road into the mountains. "Almost there," he said cheerfully. "We'll reach the cabin about half an hour before sunset."

Several minutes later he slowed down. A big tanker truck marked "Pleasant Valley Dairy" was poking along ahead of us, slowing almost to a crawl to negotiate the hairpin turns.

Lisa laughed. "We may get there half an hour before sunset *tomorrow* at this rate," she remarked. She frowned. "Where is that truck going? Where is Pleasant Valley Dairy?"

Her father shook his head. "I have no idea where the dairy is," he replied, "but this isn't the first time I've seen one of these trucks up here." He swung the van slightly into the left lane so that he could see around the truck. "We'll pass him when the road straightens out after this next curve."

Ten minutes later we topped a hill. Mr. Diamond pulled the van to the left shoulder and stopped just inches from the guardrail. "Thunderbird Lake," he said grandly. "One of the most beautiful places in all of God's creation."

We scooted to the left windows to look. He was right. Down below us, a sapphire blue lake glittered and sparkled in the late afternoon sun. The surrounding hills were blanketed in the shimmering golds, fiery reds, and brilliant oranges of an October forest. To the east of the lake, a rocky cliff rose in bold splendor for several hundred feet. A lone bird—I think it was a hawk or some kind of eagle—soared majestically in the warm air currents above the lake. The view was breath taking.

I watched for the Pleasant Valley Dairy truck—Mr. Diamond had passed it several minutes ago—but it never reappeared, and so I assumed that it had turned off somewhere. Our tires screamed as Mr. Diamond guided the van through the winding curves down the mountainside.

Lisa leaned forward in anticipation. "We're almost there, Penny! We'll be at the cabin in about three minutes." The van turned off the road and began to bounce along a narrow, rutted gravel lane.

I was excited too, but a troublesome thought suddenly nagged at me. I began to feel uneasy. *This place is going to be pretty primitive,* I told myself. *I should have asked a few questions before I agreed to come.*

"Where will we sleep?" I asked Lisa. "We won't all be in one room, will we? Will we have our own room? What about bathrooms?"

Lisa waved her hand as if to dismiss my questions. "Don't worry, Penny."

The van circled around a beautiful stand of white birches, and suddenly we were at the lake. Mr. Diamond stopped in front of a huge lodge or motel right at the water's edge. The building was an A-frame design, two stories, with a wing extending out from each side of the A-frame. The end of the building facing the lake was all glass, with a huge redwood deck extending out over the lake. Down below, at the water's edge, were a dock and a boathouse. I could see the back end of a fancy powerboat hanging in slings above the water.

I stared up at the lodge, and then turned to Lisa. "Why are we stopping here?"

Lisa smiled. "This is Daddy's cabin."

The lake was shrouded in darkness as we finished supper out on the deck over the lake. I sat back in my chair and let out a sigh of contentment. The grilled ribs had been delicious! This was going to be a good week!

I took a deep breath and looked out over the lake. This was such a peaceful place. A million stars glittered overhead, looking bigger and brighter than any I had ever seen. They seemed to be hanging in the air just a few feet above the table, and I had to resist the urge to reach up and try to touch one. The water of the lake lapped gently at the piers beneath the deck, and, out in the middle, reflected the silver beams of the moon, which was nearly full. Frogs sang to each other down in the water below the deck, and somewhere out in the darkness, a loon gave a lonely call that sent shivers up my spine.

Sherlock set his glass down on the table and pointed skyward. "Company's coming."

We all looked up. High over the lake, tiny red and white lights twinkled as a small plane circled in the darkness. Suddenly we heard the drone of the plane's engines, sounding like some kind of mechanical insect. Just then, the lights on the plane winked out. Moments later, they came back on, and then flashed on and off several times. "He's signaling somebody!" Brandon said excitedly.

In the darkness across the lake, another light began blinking on and off, as if in answer to the blinking lights of the airplane. Something very unusual was going on.

The plane dropped lower. "He's coming in for a landing," Mr. Diamond said quietly. "It sounds like a Beechcraft."

Sherlock looked at him with interest. "Do you fly?"

Mr. Diamond nodded.

As we watched, the plane's lights suddenly winked out completely. We could still hear the engines though, so we knew the plane was still there. It sounded as if the aircraft was dropping lower and lower. And then, the engines stopped.

"He's landed on the lake," Sherlock said. "He must be equipped with pontoons." I glanced at him. His eyes were wide behind his thick glasses, and I could tell that his mind was racing. He knew that something was up.

We heard the roar of a powerful boat motor, and a tiny white light went bobbing out across the water toward the spot where we figured that the plane had landed. The boat motor stopped, and the light winked out. We sat breathlessly, straining to see what was happening, but of course could see nothing in the darkness. I thought I could see the wings of the plane silhouetted in the moonlight, but it was probably just my imagination.

Two or three minutes later the boat motor roared to life again and the white light went bouncing across the water toward shore. We heard the plane engines start up, go puttering across the lake, and then seem to rise into the air. But no lights came on. Apparently the pilot did not want to be seen and was going to fly out without lights.

When the drone of the plane engines faded in the distance, Sherlock nudged me. "Something fishy is going on here," he whispered, "and we're going to find out what it is!"

I shivered as a cold feeling of danger suddenly swept over me. This was our first night at Thunderbird Lake, and we had already discovered a mystery!

THREE

EMERGENCY

I lay awake in my room that night, wondering about the mysterious plane. *What was going on here at Thunderbird Lake? Who was flying that plane, and who was on the shore signaling? Was the plane picking something up, or maybe dropping somebody off? Why didn't they do it in the daytime when it would be safer? Why did the plane come in without lights and fly back out the same way?* Something mighty strange was going on here.

Finally I climbed out of bed and tiptoed to the window. My room was on the southwest corner of the house, but if I leaned into the big bay window, I could see the area of the lake where the plane had landed. I peered eagerly into the darkness but could see nothing. All was quiet.

After several minutes I crept back to bed, trying to be as quiet as possible so I wouldn't disturb anybody. Lisa was in the room just across the hall from mine, while Mr. Diamond and the boys were in rooms farther down. As I pulled the sheet up around my chin, I thought about the huge fancy lodge we were in.

Lisa had given us a tour of the "cabin" after supper. As it turned out, there were eight bedrooms, each with its own bathroom and a Jacuzzi tub! There were three different dining rooms (two upstairs and one downstairs), two kitchens, three dens, a conference room, a weight room and sauna, a library, and two game rooms. There were three more bathrooms downstairs. Of course, every room had state-of-the-art computer equipment. This was no cabin. The place was a regular resort!

Lisa had explained that Diamond Point, as the property was called, was built for the purpose of winning people to Jesus. She told us that Mr. Diamond often brought executives and supervisors from his company, and even from other companies, up for weekend retreats. The schedule of activities always included a daily Bible study and a trip to the local Baptist church on Sunday. "Daddy always calls Pastor McClain and tells him when he'll have these people in the service, and Pastor McClain preaches a simple gospel message," she told us, her eyes shining with excitement. "Daddy has led twenty-seven people to the Lord here at Diamond Point."

I thought about that as I lay quietly in the darkness of my room. "Lord, help me learn to win people to you like Lisa and her father do," I whispered. My mind wandered back to the mysterious airplane, and I drifted off to sleep wondering what was happening at Thunderbird Lake.

The next morning we walked across the sand toward the boathouse. "Thunderbird Lake covers fourteen hundred acres," Lisa told us. "If you could see it from the top of Eagle's Nest, the cliff to the east there, you'd see that the lake is shaped almost like the outline of a bird with its wings outstretched. It's about three miles from one wingtip to the other. The head of the bird is almost due west with the wings pointing north and south.

Diamond Point is somewhere along the bottom edge of the south wing, so we're on the east side of the lake. Diamond Point and Briarwood are the only developed properties on the south wing, and there are just three small cottages on the north wing. Most of the shoreline is wilderness. It's a beautiful, quiet lake."

"What's that place there?" Brandon asked, pointing to a huge resort across the lake to the west. The property was well over half a mile away, but we could see that it was elaborate. A huge three-story building of white stone graced the hillside just above the water. Down at the water's edge, I could see a building that must have been a boathouse. A huge American flag flew over the property.

"That's Briarwood," Lisa replied. "It's right where the bird's head would be on the outline of the lake. It belongs to Senator Greene."

"Senator Adam Greene?" Sherlock asked.

Lisa nodded, and Sherlock frowned.

"Who's Senator Greene?" I asked.

Sherlock paused before answering. "He's an ultra-liberal United States senator," he finally said, "and one of the worst this country has ever had! He's an environmental extremist, and he's pushed much of the progressive, liberal legislation that is ruining our public school system. His wife has been an outspoken proponent of abortion rights. Adam Greene really shouldn't be a United States senator."

Brandon looked at Sherlock in surprise. "Wow! Sounds like you don't like the guy!"

"I've never met the senator," Sherlock replied, "but I know what he and his wife stand for. They've also been involved in one illegal business deal after another, but the liberal news media keep covering for them."

"Great!" I said. "So we have them for neighbors this week!"

"Briarwood is the senator's getaway cabin," Lisa told us, "so he may not even be here now." She slid the boathouse door open.

Brandon let out a low whistle. "Look at that baby!"

Hanging just above the water was a sleek, powerful-looking speedboat. The red fiberglass hull was accented with blue and white highlights, which included a number of diamonds. The name across the transom identified her as the *Gemstone*. The boat was pretty impressive!

"Nice boat," Sherlock observed. "What powers it?"

"It has a V-8," Lisa answered, "that develops 385 horse-power! Daddy says that the *Gemstone* will do over eighty. It's fun to drive!"

Brandon's interest was aroused. "Will he let us take her out?"

Lisa nodded. "Probably."

I glanced over to the side of the boathouse. *Now that's what I'd like to try!* I thought to myself. Hanging in slings above the water were two purple and white jet skis! I could just imagine how much fun it would be to take one of them roaring across the lake. I love jet skis! But of course I've never had the chance to try one.

Lisa seemed to read my thoughts. "Those are called wave runners," she told me. "You'll get your chance at those; that's what they're here for." She turned toward the door. "Come on, we don't want to be late for breakfast."

We hurried up to the deck where a thin little man was cooking steaks on the huge grill. He was hardly bigger than Sherlock. I was taller than he was! He turned as we approached, and I saw that he was about sixty years old. His hair was dyed jet black, but the wrinkled face gave him away. Dark blue tattoos covered both of his skinny arms. "Who are your friends, Miss Lisa?" he asked in a raspy voice that sounded almost like a chain saw.

"These are some friends from school," Lisa replied. "This is Penny Gordon, Brandon Marshall, and Sherlock Jones. They're spending the week at Diamond Point. Penny and Sherlock go to our church, and Brandon just started going. He just got saved two weeks ago." She turned toward us and gestured toward the man. "And this is Robert, Daddy's caretaker. He had last night off. He lives at Diamond Point year round, and he's the best cook on this planet!"

The little man grinned. "Careful, Miss Lisa, or you'll have me asking your father for a raise." He scanned all of us in a glance. "Pleased to make your acquaintance."

He turned his attention to Brandon. "Just got saved, did you? That's good. Now you listen to old Robert. Now that you know the Lord, you want to be careful who your friends are. Hang around people who love the Lord. Lisa Diamond and her father are some of the best Christians I know, and they can help you in your Christian life. But the wrong friends will hinder you from serving the Lord." Brandon nodded.

Robert looked at Sherlock. "Are you the lad who saved Lisa's life?"

Sherlock nodded, slightly embarrassed.

The little caretaker seized Sherlock's hand and shook it enthusiastically. "We owe you, son," he rasped. "Thanks for what you did. I know the Lord was in it, but we appreciate your part."

He turned to me. "Hi, Freckles," he said. "I hope you enjoy your stay at Diamond Point." I usually get mad when people call me "Freckles," but somehow, this little man said it in such a friendly way that I didn't resent him at all. He didn't say it to be mean.

Mr. Diamond stepped out on the deck just then. "Good morning, everyone!" he boomed. He always talks loudly, as if you were farther away than you really are. "Breakfast ready, Robert?"

"Just about, sir. Steak and eggs with cat head biscuits and jelly. Maimee is just finishing the gravy, and I'll have it all served up in a jiffy." Robert turned back to the grill and stirred a skillet of scrambled eggs.

At that moment a tiny little woman hurried out onto the deck carrying a steaming bowl of gravy. She was even shorter than Robert. Tight curls of snow white hair framed a wrinkled face with dark eyes. She set the bowl on the table.

"Kids, this little lady is Maimee Biddler, the love of my life," Robert interrupted. "She's the loveliest lady in the world, and," he threw a mischievous glance in her direction, "the world's second-best cook."

Mr. Diamond laughed.

As Robert introduced each of us to his wife, she nodded and smiled shyly, but I noticed that she didn't say a word.

I noticed a large green telescope mounted on a pedestal at the far corner of the deck. "Does that work?"

Lisa nodded. "Try it. It's incredible!"

The magic of the telescope took me right to the other side of the lake. The thing was powerful. I could see a blue jay in a pine tree that must have been a mile away. I swung the telescope toward Briarwood, the mansion belonging to Senator Greene. "You ought to see this place," I told the others. "It's fancier than the White House! There's marble columns and fountains and bushes shaped to look like animals, and . . . Hey, there's a big motor home! Down close to the lake across from the boat-house."

Sherlock took a look through the instrument. "It's a brand new diesel," he reported. "That's a half-million dollar rig!" He swung the telescope along the shoreline. "The lake looks like it ends just north of the senator's place," he said, "but it must continue around the bend."

"It does," Lisa told him. "We can just see the south wing of the Thunderbird from here, which is less than half of the lake."

"Come and get it!" a raspy voice shouted, and we hurried over to indulge ourselves in Robert's cooking. It was one terrific breakfast. Lisa was right!

"I want some time alone to do some thinking and planning," Mr. Diamond told Lisa as we finished breakfast. "You can take the gang out on the *Gemstone*, try out the wave runners, do some hiking, or whatever you want. Just be sure to stay together, and I want life jackets on anyone who goes on the water. We'll meet back here for lunch."

"It's not too cool to try the jet skis," I said hopefully. "This is awfully warm for October."

"It is unusually warm," Sherlock agreed. "This is called Indian summer."

"Native American summer," Lisa corrected him with a mischievous grin. "It's not politically correct to say Indian summer."

"Oh, brother," Mr. Diamond remarked. "And to think we used to play 'Cowboys and Indians' when we were kids. I suppose we should have played 'Cowboys and Native Americans.' "

"Not really," Sherlock said, continuing the jesting. "The term cowboys could be interpreted as derogatory. You should have played 'Beef Production Engineers and Native Americans'. Or maybe the game should be called 'Bovine Guidance Specialists and Native Americans.' "

Mr. Diamond shook his head. "I give up," he laughed. "Let's just enjoy the Indian summer while it's here." He looked at me. "Did you call your folks last night and tell them that we got in safely?"

I shook my head. "I forgot."

He handed me a phone. "Go ahead and make the call." He leaned over and hugged Lisa. "Mom called and said to tell you that she loves you. I've got to get working. See you at lunch." He stood up and hurried to the door.

I studied the buttons on the phone for several seconds. "How do I turn this thing on?" I asked Lisa.

"Just push the 'talk' button," she told me. "Wait for a dial tone and then dial."

The phone in my hand rang suddenly, and it scared me so badly that I dropped it. I picked it up off the table and pushed the 'talk' button. "Hello?"

A woman's voice, somewhere between a scream and a wail, blasted right in my ear. The caller was crying and trying to talk, and I couldn't understand a thing she was saying. "Ma'am, slow down please," I begged. "I can't understand you!"

The woman on the other end began to sob. She let out another wail and then began talking at warp speed again. I struggled to understand her. I caught the words "baby," "poison," and "Melissa," and suddenly realized that this was some sort of emergency. "Get your dad!" I screamed at Lisa. "There's a woman on the phone who needs help!"

Lisa dashed for the door, and I followed close behind with the phone. Sherlock made it through the door ahead of me. He darted to a phone in the entryway, lifted the receiver, and then punched a button.

The woman's voice wailed out of a speaker, and I realized that Sherlock had put the call on the speakerphone feature. "Help me, please!" the woman wailed.

Mr. Diamond ran into the room. "This is Larry Diamond," he boomed. "I'll try to help you! Who are you, and what is the problem?"

The woman choked back a sob. "Mr. Diamond, this is Tina Lewis." Apparently she was calming down a little because she was speaking more slowly and her words were more coherent. "Melissa swallowed some poison, and I'm not sure what it was! I tried to call the Poison Control Center, but I can't get through. It will take twenty minutes for an ambulance to get here. What should I do?"

Mr. Diamond turned to Maimee. "Tell Robert to fire up the *Gemstone*. Tell him it's an emergency! Hurry!" Maimee ran from the room, and he turned back to the phone. He asked the woman a couple of questions and then said, "Tina, we'll be there in about three minutes. We'll see what we can do."

He dashed from the house and raced down to the boathouse with Sherlock, Brandon, Lisa, and me right on his heels. Robert had just lowered the speedboat into the water and was cranking the engine when we dashed in. The powerful engine rumbled to life with a roar.

"I'll take it!" Mr. Diamond called to Robert. "Call Lifeline and have them get a helicopter to the Lewis place! I'll cover the costs if necessary!"

I looked at Sherlock. "But the ambulance is already on its way," I said. "It will get here by the time they get a helicopter into the air and over here."

"Yes, but the ambulance will take twenty minutes going back out," Sherlock reminded me. "The helicopter will take less than two."

Mr. Diamond was now in the boat, and he gunned the engine to half throttle. "Kids!" he called. "Come with me! Maybe you can help!" We all leaped over the side, and he put the *Gemstone* in gear and backed carefully from the boathouse. "Hang on!" When he was clear of the boathouse he shoved the throttle down hard. The prow lifted, and the boat shot forward.

Within three seconds we were shooting across the lake, going faster than I had ever gone in a boat before. It was scary. The wind whipped my hair straight back. Spray shot from both sides of the boat, and the hull began to pound up and down. We were going so fast that I thought if he turned that wheel just a tiny bit, the boat would roll over and then tumble end over end.

"Help that little girl, Lord," Mr. Diamond prayed aloud.

He looked over at Sherlock, who was seated beside him. "Melissa is just a toddler," he shouted, "probably not more than two or three. They live around the bend of the lake, less than two miles from us." He pushed the throttle down even farther and the *Gemstone* went even faster. I was terrified.

The speedboat thundered toward the narrow part of the lake. We passed within two hundred yards of the senator's elegant property. As we rounded the bend and entered the "body" of the Thunderbird, I looked back. Diamond Point was already nearly a mile away. Moments later Mr. Diamond cut the throttle as the boat approached the shore, heading straight for a small, white house about a hundred yards from the water's edge. He cut the engine completely and let the boat slide up on the beach, and then he was over the side and into the shallow water even before the *Gemstone* stopped moving. "Come on!" he yelled at us. "We'll worry about the boat later!"

The four of us scrambled from the boat and raced after the tall millionaire. He ran to the house and threw open the front door without knocking. A woman was down on the floor on her knees, clutching a trembling, screaming child in her arms. The woman looked up as we entered, and we could see that she was nearly in hysterics.

Mr. Diamond was at her side instantly. "Let me have her," he ordered. "I'll try to calm her down."

The woman handed the little girl to him.

"Lisa, why don't you try to get Poison Control on the phone?" Sherlock said. He touched the woman on the arm. "Where did Melissa find anything toxic?"

"I don't know," Mrs. Lewis wailed. "She came in the front door crying. I think she came from the garage. She said, 'Mommy I drinked it, and it hurted my tummy.' That's all I could get her to tell me. I tried immediately to call Poison Control."

Sherlock was already running out the door. "Penny! Come with me!" he called. Brandon and I followed him to the garage.

My heart sank as I viewed the interior of the garage. Against one wall was a well-organized workbench with a vise mounted at one end. The wall was covered with tools, all neatly displayed on hooks. But above the workbench were two shelves loaded with poisonous substances! Paint thinners, insecticides, solvents—you name it, and if it was toxic, it was there. Down beneath the workbench I saw two one-gallon bottles of automotive antifreeze, several plastic bottles of motor oil, and a can of brake fluid. This garage contained dozens of different items that could poison a child, and there would be no way to figure out in time which one Melissa had swallowed!

Sherlock spent about ten seconds looking over the assortment of chemicals and then started for the garage door. "It wasn't anything in here."

I grabbed his arm. "Sherlock, it could have been any of these things!" I shrilled. "Look! Paint thinner! Insecticide! Varnish! Varnish remover! Motor oil! We have to find out which one it was!"

"It wasn't any of the substances in here," Sherlock insisted. "We have to look elsewhere."

"But how do you know?" I argued. "You didn't even take the time to check it out."

"Penny, I don't have time to explain right now," he declared. "You'll have to trust me." He started to push past me, and I stepped hurriedly out of his way.

He ran back into the house with Brandon and me right behind him. "Mrs. Lewis," he said urgently, "please think quickly! Have you or your husband used any chemicals outside in the past few days?"

"Richard was stripping paint from a chair on the deck Saturday," the distraught mother answered. "But he didn't leave anything out. I already checked!"

Sherlock was already out the door again, so I dashed after him. We ran past the open garage door and around the end of the house to the back yard. Sherlock dashed to the ground-level deck against the back of the house and quickly looked it over. But there were no chemicals present. The deck was bare except for a gas grill, a picnic table, and a battered old chair. Sherlock seemed frustrated. "Nothing," he said despondently.

Suddenly his eyes lit up, and he darted to the corner of the house. While Brandon and I looked on in astonishment, Sherlock squatted down and duckwalked back toward the deck. With a cry of delight he leaped up and ran to the deck, and then dropped to his knees in the grass beside it. "This is it, Penny!" he shouted. Reaching under the edge of the deck, he pulled out a huge plastic drink cup with one hand and a gallon can of paint remover with the other. A piece of plastic food wrap fell to the ground. He tipped the cup over, and a small amount of thick, amber liquid streaked with white poured from the cup.

Handing the cup to me, he spun the can around and scanned the back of the label. "Methanol!" he shouted. He leaped to his feet and dashed into the house. I tried to keep up.

Sherlock seized the telephone from Lisa's grasp. "Is this Poison Control? Good! The child has apparently ingested some paint remover. The active ingredient is methanol. What procedure should we follow?"

He listened intently for several seconds and then said, "Thank you. Yes, I'll have someone stay on the line."

"Syrup of ipecac!" he shouted to Mrs. Lewis. "They want us to give her syrup of ipecac! Do you have any?"

"In the medicine cabinet in the bathroom!" the distraught mother shouted.

Sherlock dashed to the bathroom and returned with a tiny brown bottle. Mr. Diamond propped Melissa up in a sitting position as Sherlock twisted off the cap. Mrs. Lewis placed the bottle to her daughter's lips and stroked her throat in an attempt to get her to swallow. "Come on, baby," she begged, "drink it for Mommy!"

Melissa's eyelids fluttered, and she began to swallow. "That's it, sweetheart!" her mother coaxed. "Drink it all. That's a good girl."

Brandon and I stood nervously nearby, watching the frightening scene. Melissa was so little! I began to pray.

"Get a large dish or a pan from the kitchen," Sherlock instructed me. "This stuff is to make her vomit."

I returned with a large plastic popcorn bowl and a towel just in time. "The syrup of ipecac is working," Sherlock reported to the person on the other end of the line. He paused and then said, "No, ma'am. The ambulance is not here yet."

We waited anxiously for another ten or twelve minutes before we finally heard the sound of a siren. I let out a sigh of relief. Help was here at last! Brandon ran outside to assist the ambulance personnel in finding us.

Two EMTs in blue jackets came bursting through the door. The man carried a stretcher, and the woman had an emergency medical kit. "What did she swallow?" the man asked, kneeling on the floor beside Mrs. Lewis, who held Melissa in her lap.

"Methanol," Sherlock answered from the doorway. "We gave her syrup of ipecac."

"Good," the EMT responded. He took the trembling child from her mother and laid her gently on the sofa. The woman EMT knelt beside him, and working together, they took her vital signs. "That may have saved her life, but she's still in danger. We need to get her to the hospital as fast as possible."

At that moment, I heard the *Whup! Whup! Whup!* of a helicopter rotor overhead. "The chopper's here!" I cried. Several of us ran outside. A blue-and-white helicopter was dropping gently into the front yard. The downdraft from the rotor flattened the grass in the yard and made the bushes along the house dance in unison like cobras under the influence of a snake charmer's flute. The helicopter skids touched down, and an EMT jumped from the craft and dashed toward us.

Just then, the two EMTs inside the house carried the stretcher through the front door. Strapped in the center, looking tiny and frail and white, was little Melissa Lewis. Her mother hurried along beside the stretcher, holding one of Melissa's tiny hands. In less time than it takes to tell it, Melissa and her mother were inside the helicopter. The engine roared and whined as the emergency craft lifted into the air. We watched in silence as it disappeared over the roof of the house.

The woman EMT carried her medical kit from the house, and Mr. Diamond locked the house for Mrs. Lewis. Sherlock turned to the man from the ambulance. "How is she?" he asked worriedly. "Will she make it?"

"Methanol is pretty vicious stuff," the EMT said gravely, "with an extremely high toxicity rating. She's pretty little, which doesn't help the situation. But there's good news—methanol works very slowly. If you got her to vomit it up before it had a chance to work, she'll be OK. They'll pump her stomach at the hospital, and they'll check her blood for traces of the methanol. Let's just hope for the best." He and his partner strode to the ambulance, switched off the flashing lights, and drove from the yard.

It had all happened so fast that I really didn't have time to think about what was happening, but now that the emergency was basically over, my emotions overwhelmed me. I burst into tears. "Dear God," I sobbed quietly as we followed Mr. Diamond to the *Gemstone*, "please help little Melissa! Please, God, let her live!"

FOUR

PEARL PENDERGRASS

"So how did you know that Melissa hadn't swallowed any of the poisons in the garage?" I asked Sherlock as Mr. Diamond's speedboat thundered back across the lake. "We weren't in the garage for more than ten seconds! How could you be so sure?"

"The first thing I noticed in the garage was how well Mr. Lewis had everything organized," Sherlock replied, gripping the railing of the *Gemstone* to keep his balance. "Every tool was hanging perfectly straight, and all the containers on the shelves were lined in meticulous rows that didn't vary by a sixteenth of an inch. When I saw that all the containers were lined up perfectly, I knew that no toddler had touched them. But there was more evidence than that: every single container was tightly capped. If a two-year-old had opened a container and taken a drink of a chemical that began to cramp her stomach, would she have replaced the lid properly, even if she were capable of doing so? Hardly!"

I nodded. "OK. That make sense."

"But there was more," Sherlock continued. "Those two things together told me that Melissa hadn't tampered with the chemicals in the garage, but I had to have more proof than that. When I examined the workbench and saw that there was no way for a toddler to have climbed up on it, I knew that the containers on the shelves were completely out of the picture. Melissa simply could not have reached them."

"What about the stuff on the floor under the workbench?" I asked.

"That was the only other option," Sherlock replied, "but one glance told me that she could not have gotten into any of those."

"How did you know that?" I argued.

"Do you remember what was down there?" the young detective responded with a question of his own.

"Uh, let's see," I said, trying to remember. "Uh, there was some motor oil, and, uh, some other stuff for cars, I think."

"Right," Sherlock agreed. "There were two one-gallon jugs of automotive antifreeze, three quarts of oil, and a can of brake fluid."

"But all of those are poisonous!" I stated.

"True, but they had not been disturbed by Melissa."

"But how could you tell?" I asked, just a bit frustrated. Sherlock notices details that the average person never even sees, and I knew that he had picked up on some clue that I had overlooked. Since I started hanging around Sherlock, I've tried and tried to learn to be observant like he is, but it's no use. He may be the one wearing the thick glasses, but he sees stuff that I never notice. Compared to him, I'm a little old lady with cataracts.

"The two plastic jugs of antifreeze have those childproof caps that adults can barely open," he told me. "Ever try to open one? There's no way a two-year-old could do it! The bottles of motor oil had never been opened; the plastic rings around the caps were still intact. And the can of brake fluid still had the original seal around the lid."

I shook my head. As usual, it all fit together and made sense when he explained it. Why couldn't I learn to notice details and think things through like he did? I sometimes feel as if my brain is an old 286 computer with one megabyte of RAM, while Sherlock's brain is a state-of-the-art computer with more RAM than he would ever need! And don't think it's just because he's a boy and I'm a girl. That has nothing to do with it!

Another question popped into my busy head. "Remember when we looked around the deck and didn't find anything? Why did you get down and duckwalk from the corner of the house?"

He grinned. "It worked, didn't it? I was just trying to see things from Melissa's perspective."

Lisa, Brandon and Mr. Diamond had been listening to all this without comment, and now Mr. Diamond spoke up. "Thank the Lord you were able to find the paint remover so quickly. From what the EMT was telling me, little Melissa has a pretty good chance since we got her to vomit the methanol so soon after she swallowed it."

Sherlock shook his head. "I just hope the Lewises will be more careful. People who live that close to a lake should never let a toddler go outside without supervision, anyway."

My eyes misted up with tears as I thought of what could have happened. We still didn't know if Melissa was going to be all right, but she might have died if it hadn't been for Sherlock. *Thank you, Lord,* I prayed silently, *for equipping Sherlock with such a brilliant mind. His ability to notice details and think swiftly may have saved Melissa's life!*

I looked up to notice that we were speeding past Briarwood. Just to the north of the senator's elegant property, the shoreline cut in sharply, forming a little cove. The inlet was probably two or three hundred yards across. "Is that the head of the thunder-bird?" I guessed.

"Right," Lisa told me. "Senator Greene considers it his personal property, so we never go in there." She glanced up toward the mansion. "Hey! There he is now!"

A tall, dignified man in golf clothes was standing on the pier beside the boathouse. He lifted one hand in a casual wave as we sped past, so we waved back. "So he is home," Brandon remarked.

Lisa nodded.

Mr. Diamond cut the engine as we approached Diamond Point. Robert and his wife were waiting at the dock. "How's the little girl?" they asked anxiously. "Is she all right?"

Mr. Diamond shook his head. "It's too early to tell, but the ambulance personnel seemed to think she was going to make it. Sherlock found the poison that she had swallowed, and we were able to help her in time. I'll tell you about it while we put the *Gemstone* away."

Brandon, Lisa, Sherlock and I stepped off at the dock, and the little caretaker stepped aboard. Mr. Diamond put the *Gemstone* in gear and motored slowly into the boathouse.

Lisa turned to us. "There's someone I want you to meet," she said. "Her name is Pearl Pendergrass, and she lives on a little farm just over the hill behind Diamond Point."

My heart sank. *I'm dying to try the wave runners, and now Lisa wants to take us to visit a friend!* But I was too polite to insist on having my own way or even mention it right then, for that matter. *If this girl is anything like Lisa, it will be worth waiting for the wave runners,* I grudgingly told myself. *Be patient, Penny!*

I couldn't help letting out a quiet sigh as we walked toward the cabin. Patience is not one of my stronger points, and I wanted to try those wave runners so bad! "Badly," I guess I should say. Sorry, Miss Wiggins!

The morning was already getting rather warm, so we stopped at the cabin for some cold cans of soft drink. The Diamonds' lodge is about ten times as big as my whole house, and I feel funny calling it a cabin, but that's what Lisa calls it, so I guess I will too.

We sipped the soft drinks as we hiked over the hill following a narrow footpath that wound its way through the woods behind Diamond Point. Sherlock was in front of me, and he suddenly stopped and pointed. "Look!" he whispered. *"Danaus plexippus!"*

Lisa spun around and stared at Sherlock. "What did you say?" she asked. She was looking at him as if he had just said a bad word.

"Danaus plexippus," Sherlock repeated. "I'm sorry, I should have just said that it was a Monarch."

Brandon took a sip of his soft drink. "What's a Monarch?"

"It's a butterfly," I sighed. "Sherlock has this thing with insects, and especially with butterflies." I suddenly realized that Lisa and Brandon hadn't been around Sherlock as much as I had, and they weren't aware of his obsession with butterflies. He wants to be an entomologist, somebody that studies insects. To me, that seems like a perfect waste of his fantastic mind. Imagine Edison spending his life studying fruit flies, or Einstein making a career of ladybugs!

"Where's the Monarch?" Lisa asked. "I don't see any butterfly."

"Up there," the would-be-entomologist replied, pointing. "In the branches of that ailanthus, about fifteen feet from the ground."

Lisa studied the tree that Sherlock indicated. "OK, I see it."

"So what's so special about a butterfly?" Brandon demanded. "When you've seen one, you've seen 'em all."

Sherlock shrugged. "They present a fascinating study," he answered. "Take this Monarch, for example. Did you know that Monarchs are migratory and sometimes travel more than two thousand miles to reach warmer climates when cold weather threatens? They usually travel in huge swarms with thousands and thousands of fellow travelers. This little fellow must have strayed from the swarm."

Brandon threw a rock at the butterfly, missing by three or four inches. "Better get moving!" he called to the beautiful creature. "Winter's just around the corner!"

Lisa gazed at Sherlock. "How did you know that that tree is an ailanthus?" she asked. "Most visitors that Daddy brings up here don't know a pine from an oak!"

Sherlock looked sheepish. "I wasn't really very well versed on my flora until last night," he admitted, "but I found *Patterson's Field Guide to Trees* in your dad's library and assimilated some data so I wouldn't appear totally ignorant in the woods."

Lisa looked puzzled. "You did what with the book?"

. "He memorized it," I explained. "Probably in one sitting."

Brandon looked amazed. "Unbelievable!"

"The ailanthus, or *Ailanthus altissima*, is actually native to China," Sherlock said, looking back at the greenish yellow tree with the butterfly resting in it, "but it now ranges across the eastern United States and southeastern Canada. It normally grows to a height of fifty or sixty feet but can reach heights of a hundred feet, often growing as rapidly as eight feet per year."

"OK, Mr. Botanist, let's quiz you," Lisa said mischievously. She pointed to a pale yellow tree close to the trail. "What's that?"

"That's a northern hackberry," Sherlock told her, "also known as *Celtis occidentalis*."

I stared at him. "Did you memorize the Latin names too?"

He shrugged. "They were in the book." He reached up and picked a leaf from the hackberry tree. "This tree grows to a height of thirty to seventy feet and ranges across the northeastern quarter of the United States and parts of southern Canada. It flowers in April and May."

"What about that one?" Brandon challenged, pointing to a tree with bronze-colored leaves farther down the trail.

"European horsechestnut," Sherlock replied. "The Latin name is *Aesculus hippocastanum*. It was introduced from Europe and now covers much of the U.S. and southeastern Canada. It can range from twenty-five to seventy-five feet in height. In May it has long clusters of white flowers. The thorny fruit you see appears in September."

We quizzed him on several more trees and other plants, and he knew them all, giving us the common name, the Latin name, and other information such as average height and reproduction cycle. I even came back to one that we had already asked him, just to see if he was making it all up as he went along, but he recited exactly the same information as he did the first time.

Brandon shook his head and gave Sherlock an admiring glance as we started up the trail again. "Man, what I couldn't do with a brain like yours!"

"I'm grateful for what God has given me," Sherlock replied, "and I always try to use it appropriately. That's why I never waste my time with television or video games."

"You don't watch *any* TV?" I croaked. This was news! I couldn't imagine life without a bit of TV now and then!

"Television fills your mind with useless and often harmful information," Sherlock replied, "and video games are a waste of time. Educators are telling us that video games hinder a young person's mental development, retard his academic potential, and hamper his performance in various intellectual pursuits."

"I can't imagine giving up TV!" I exclaimed.

Sherlock shrugged. "You'd do better in school if you did, Penny," he chided. "I'm just trying to be a good steward of the mental faculties with which God has endowed me. We all should."

I took a sip of my soft drink and thought about it as we hiked along. *A steward of the mind God has given me?* I never thought about it in that way before.

To my surprise, the forest gave way to a clearing less than five hundred yards from Mr. Diamond's cabin. As we hiked over the crest of the hill, we found ourselves at the edge of a picturesque farm snuggled in a gentle valley between two rolling hills. To our left stood a field of corn—tall, brown, and ready for harvest. I could just imagine the fun that we could have if the owner would permit us to have a cornstalk battle in there. The field to our right was planted in soybeans, which stood only knee-high even though they were also ready for harvest. An ancient farmhouse squatted on the dividing line between the two crops, with a huge, faded red barn behind it. The barn leaned to one side, giving the impression that one sneeze from a butterfly might blow it right over. I saw a chicken house just to the east of the barn. A lazy, shallow river flowed along one edge of the clearing. The place looked like a picture you would see on a postcard. You could tell that the farm was old, but it was really pretty.

Lisa grabbed two strands of the barbed wire fence in front of us and held them apart for us to climb through. "After you," she said.

We followed her down the hill through the soybeans. When we approached the house, we had to walk through a flock of large reddish-brown chickens, which were busily pecking around in the yard. I was surprised to see an old-fashioned iron pump in the front yard, surrounded by a bed of bright pink flowers. Even more of a surprise was the little building between the house and the barn. It was less than four feet square, and I knew immediately what it was.

"They still use a pump?" I observed. "And an outhouse? Don't they have running water?"

"The pump and the outhouse both still work," Lisa replied, "but she does have running water."

A slender, elderly lady with little round glasses stepped out on the porch just then. Her thinning, snow-white hair made me think of a dandelion when it's ready for you to blow all the little seed parachutes off. She looked friendly.

The woman's eyes lit up when she saw us standing there. "It seems that I have visitors," she said with a note of delight in her voice. "And who might you be?" And then she recognized Lisa. "Lisa Diamond," she exclaimed, "I haven't seen you in a long time! Who are your friends?"

"Mrs. Pendergrass," Lisa said politely, "I want you to meet some friends of mine. This is Penny Gordon, Brandon Marshall, and Sherlock Jones. I go to school with them. The school board gave us some unexpected time off from school, so we're spending the week up here with Daddy."

Mrs. Pendergrass smiled at us as if we were the best things that had ever happened to her. "It's a pleasure to meet you," she told us eagerly. "I do hope you can stay awhile." She turned to Lisa. "It's sure good to see you again, sweetheart."

"Do come in," our elderly hostess invited now that the introductions had been made. "I just took a batch of cookies from the oven not more than fifteen minutes ago." She chuckled and looked at Lisa. "I made them to take to Pastor McClain Wednesday night, but I guess he'll get what's left, right?"

We followed Mrs. Pendergrass into a tiny, old-fashioned kitchen, and I noticed that she smelled like cinnamon. She had a refrigerator and stove and all that, but they looked like they were at least forty years old. There was no microwave or dishwasher. We sat at a little round table in the corner, under a huge hand-lettered plaque.

I stared up at the plaque on the wall above the table. The letters had been burned into the wood and spelled out Matthew 6:21, "For where your treasure is, there will your heart be also."

Mrs. Pendergrass placed a plate of warm snickerdoodle cookies on the table and noticed my interest in the plaque. "My husband made that for me the day he died," she said softly. "Someday I'll tell you the story behind it."

Little old ladies always seem to think that you need milk with your cookies, and Mrs. Pendergrass was no exception. In no time at all she had set four canning jars on the table in front of us and filled them with milk, even though we each still had a can of soft drink sitting in front of us. She drew a stool up close to the table and perched on it and then reached for a cookie.

Trying not to be too obvious, I studied the old woman as I bit into my first cookie. Judging by the white hair and the wrinkles, I'd guess that she was somewhere around seventy-five or eighty years old. But she moved with the energy and grace of a woman half that age, and she sat on the stool like a teenager, with her feet wrapped around the legs. *Either she's not as old as she looks,* I told myself, *or she's in awfully good shape for being as old as she is!*

"Who runs the farm?" The question came from Brandon. He's never been known to be bashful.

Mrs. Pendergrass smiled. "I do. George died more than sixty years ago, and I've been alone ever since." She smiled again. "I guess I should say that the Lord and I run it. I couldn't go a day without Him."

"Your husband died sixty years ago?" I echoed. "How old was—uh . . ." I stopped, realizing how personal and impolite my question would have sounded.

"How old was he?" The old lady chuckled. "You're trying to figure out how old I am, right?"

Was I embarrassed! My skin felt hot, and if I could have seen my face, I'm sure it was beet red under all those freckles.

"That's quite all right, honey," Mrs. Pendergrass reassured me with a laugh. "George was only twenty-two when we married, and I was twenty. We had only been married three years when he died." She patted my arm. "So do your math and tell me how old I am."

"You're over eighty," I said, and she nodded.

"And you run this farm?" Brandon said in disbelief. "Who does the plowing? And the . . . well, whatever else you do on a farm."

"I do it myself, thank you," came the spirited reply. "I'm still spry enough to climb aboard a tractor. The only time I need help is when it's time to bring in the harvest, and that's only because I don't own a combine. I hire a neighbor to do that for me."

Mrs. Pendergrass turned to Lisa. "I heard the mail come just before you arrived," she said. "How about running out to check it for me? I was just heading out to do it when you showed up, and I guess I plumb forgot all about it."

Lisa stood to her feet. "I'll be glad to, Mrs. Pendergrass." She hurried from the room, and I reached for another cookie.

Brandon and Sherlock were teasing each other about who had already eaten the most cookies, but I paid them no attention. These things were delicious!

Lisa was back in less time than it would take a bald man to comb his hair. "You only got one letter, Mrs. Pendergrass," she said, handing an envelope to the old lady, "but it's from the APE."

Sherlock looked up with interest. "The APE?" he said. "Why would they be writing you?"

Brandon frowned. "What's the ape? Sounds like King Kong or something."

"Not ape," Sherlock responded patiently, "A-P-E. That stands for 'Administration Protecting the Environment'. The APE is a state-level regulatory agency modeled after the EPA. The EPA is a federal agency that sets policy regarding the use of our natural resources and supposedly makes sure that the environment is not harmed or threatened. But many scientists say that a large percentage of the EPA's regulations and rulings are based on faulty research and shoddy science and are totally unnecessary. Economists estimate that the unnecessary regulations alone cost our nation several hundred billion dollars each year."

Brandon frowned again. "That's a lot of money."

Sherlock nodded.

Mrs. Pendergrass had opened the envelope and was reading the letter. The color drained from her face, and her hands began to shake. "Oh my!" she exclaimed.

Lisa was at her side in a flash. "Mrs. Pendergrass! What's wrong?"

The elderly lady shook her head. "Nothing for you to worry about, child. This is just a matter that I have to take up with my Lord."

"But can we help?" Lisa coaxed. "Is there something Daddy can do?"

Mrs. Pendergrass stood slowly to her feet. "Thank you, sweetheart, but there's really nothing you can do." She smiled at all of us. "Thank you for dropping in, but I'm afraid that right now I need to be alone with my Lord. Please do come again. Maybe tomorrow?"

We picked up our soft drinks and headed for the door. "Thanks for the cookies, Mrs. Pendergrass," Brandon said, reaching out to grab two more as he passed the table. "They were fantastic!"

We left Mrs. Pendergrass sitting at the kitchen table with her head bowed over the letter from the APE. I had no idea what was in the letter, but I could tell from her face that it must have been something really awful. I worried about it as we hurried through the woods toward Diamond Point. I just knew that something really bad was about to happen to a sweet, innocent old lady.

FIVE

NIGHT FISHING

"That old lady is really nice," Brandon said as we hiked back toward Diamond Point. "I liked her. And she bakes a mean cookie!"

"Mrs. Pendergrass is one of the sweetest, godliest people I've ever known," Lisa replied. "You know what she told me one day? She was saved when she was five years old. That means that she's known the Lord for over seventy-five years!"

"Three quarters of a century," Sherlock said softly. A sober look crossed his face, and suddenly he was deep in thought.

"What's on your mind?" I asked him.

"I'm just wondering what was in that letter she got from the APE," he replied, swinging his stick at a tree branch across the trail. "Whatever it was, you could see that it really upset her."

"She'll tell us about it when she's ready," Lisa told us, "but not before."

"How about if we get the wave runners out?" I suggested as we reached Diamond Point. "I'm just dying to try them!"

Lisa laughed. "Sure, Penny," she agreed. "I'll get Robert to put them in the water for us."

Five minutes later I was seated on the back of a snarling wave runner, hanging on for dear life as Lisa did her best to sling me off. The little watercraft sounded like a motorcycle and accelerated almost as fast as one. Trying to catch me off guard, Lisa gunned the wave runner at full throttle and then threw it into a tight turn. The nose of the wave runner dropped and the back end suddenly lifted and flung itself around sideways. It was all I could do to stay on the seat. She did it several times. I was grateful for the life vest strapped securely over my shirt.

Brandon came racing by us on the other wave runner. Sherlock was on the back, and it didn't look like he was enjoying the ride. He wasn't wearing his glasses—I had never seen him without them before—and his eyes were tightly closed. Brandon is so big and Sherlock is so small that together they looked like a father-son combination. A stranger watching them would never have guessed that they were in the same grade at school.

Lisa and Brandon raced the wave runners across the lake to Briarwood and back again. Lisa eased up on the throttle and headed for the boathouse. When we pulled up to the dock, she looked over her shoulder at me. "Want to drive it?"

"Sure!" I responded. "I was hoping you would offer."

She laughed and stepped off onto the dock. "Go to it!"

I scooted forward and grabbed the handlebars. Lisa looked at Brandon, who had brought the other wave runner alongside ours. "Why don't you let Sherlock drive that one?" Brandon idled the craft alongside the dock and stepped off, and Sherlock scooted forward and took the controls. He pulled his glasses from his pocket and put them on.

"Take them to the north side of the lake for a few minutes if you want," Lisa called. "Just be sure not to get too close to shore. The intake will suck up sand, mud, and rocks, and that can damage the impellers! Have a good ride!"

"Race you to the north end!" I shouted at Sherlock. Hoping to get a head start, I mashed my thumb down hard on the throttle lever. The wave runner leaped forward with more power than I expected, and I wasn't ready for it. I was speeding straight for the side of the boathouse! I panicked! Forgetting to let up on the throttle, I jerked the handlebars to the left, and the wave runner spun around in a tight circle to the left. I wasn't ready for that either, and the force of the turn threw me hard to the right. In terror I looked up to realize that I was speeding straight for the dock! With less than a second to spare, I jerked the handlebars around to the right, missing the end of the dock by less than a yard. The maneuver threw me hard to the left, but at least I avoided a collision with the dock, which would have demolished the wave runner and maybe me. I came within a gnat's whisker of falling off, but I finally remembered to let up on the throttle. The wave runner drifted to a stop, and my wake caught up with me, abruptly lifting the rear of the craft and again nearly spilling me off.

Sherlock went shooting past me. "See ya, Penny!" Here I was about to kill myself on this ornery machine, and he didn't even stop to help! His wave runner went zipping across the lake like a racehorse going into the home stretch. Sherlock was leaning forward like a world-class jockey.

"Oh, no, you don't!" I muttered. I twisted the handlebars straight and thumbed the throttle, a little slower and more carefully this time. The engine growled and my steed rose up in the water and went galloping after Sherlock's. I thumbed the throttle down harder, and the little craft shot across the water.

When we reached the narrow part of the lake, Sherlock put his wave runner into a wide turn. But I cut straight across, determined to catch up. As he entered the north wing of the Thunderbird, he glanced over his shoulder and saw that I was gaining on him. But then to my disappointment, he slowed down to let me catch up. Sometimes Sherlock is just not competitive. In seconds, my little craft was alongside his.

"These are a lot more fun when you get to drive them yourself, aren't they?" he shouted. "Let's take them across to the northernmost tip of the lake."

We both thumbed the throttles at the same time, and the wave runners responded in unison, leaping forward like eager racehorses. The wind whipped my hair straight back and made the edges of my culottes flap like birds' wings. My craft bucked up and down under me as it crossed tiny waves on the surface of the lake. It was fun!

It took about three minutes to reach the north end of the lake. An island less than a hundred yards long loomed ahead of us, with a hundred-foot wide channel between it and the shore. Sherlock guided his craft around the end of the island and into the channel, so I followed him. I wasn't sure if the water would be deep enough for the wave runners, but I figured if it was too shallow, Sherlock would find out about it first.

As we flew around the end of the island, we startled a man who had been fishing in the channel. He looked up with an expression of panic and, to my surprise, dropped his fishing rod and ran for the woods. There was an open space of about fifty yards between the water and the edge of the forest, and the man raced across as if a bear was chasing him. Twice I saw him look back over his shoulder as he ran, but he never slowed down even though he must have seen that we were just kids. It didn't make sense to me.

Sherlock turned his wave runner in a circle on the other side of the channel, and I caught up with him. He slowed as I came alongside. "Did you see that man?" I shouted.

Sherlock nodded. He let the wave runner drop back to an idle, and I did the same.

"What was he afraid of?" I asked Sherlock. "Did you see his face? When he saw us, he looked like he was terrified!"

"His response indicates that either he's afraid of someone, or for some reason he doesn't want to be seen," Sherlock replied. "Come on. Let's run through the channel again." He gunned his wave runner in a tight circle and shot straight for the channel, so I followed suit.

We powered through the channel again, but there was no sign of the frightened fisherman. When we reached the spot where we had seen him, Sherlock brought his wave runner to a stop, and I barely got mine stopped in time to keep from ramming him. These things need brake lights. Sherlock pointed at the bank where the man had stood. "He came back!"

"How can you tell?" I asked.

"The fishing rod is gone."

I looked, and sure enough, Sherlock was right. In the few seconds that we had been out on the lake, the man had returned and retrieved his fishing rod.

Sherlock drove the wave runner close to shore. "I'm going to check it out."

A cold feeling of apprehension swept over me. "Sherlock, don't!" I begged. "Let's get out of here! What if he comes back? What if he's a dangerous criminal? Maybe he was fishing without a license and is afraid of being caught. Desperate people do violent things when they're cornered!"

He ignored me and hopped off the wave runner. Leaving the craft bobbing gently in the shallow water, he ran across to the point where the mysterious man had been fishing. He knelt and examined the ground for several seconds, and then he stood and quickly scanned the area. To my chagrin, he walked toward the woods where the man had disappeared. I waited apprehensively. What if the man did come back?

Sherlock was back in less than a minute, but it seemed like an eternity. To my surprise, he was carrying a red soda pop can. He knelt at the water's edge and drained several ounces of soda into the water, and then waded back to the wave runner. I noticed he was handling the can carefully, holding it by the top rim. When he reached the wave runner he lifted the seat and placed the can inside a storage compartment, snapped the seat closed, and then pushed the craft toward deeper water. Leaping aboard, he squeezed the throttle and guided the wave runner back through the channel. I followed.

When we were back out on the main part of the lake, Sherlock gunned his machine to full throttle, and I did the same. Within seconds, we were speeding across the water faster than anyone had ever gone until the twentieth century. I thought about what had just happened. *Who was that man? Why was he so frantic about getting away from us? Was he doing something illegal, or was he just afraid of someone? And if he was afraid of someone, why did he take the risk of coming back for the fishing rod? What was going on? Something's up,* I told myself, *because Sherlock thought it was important enough to stop!* I thought about the soft-drink can. *What was Sherlock going to do with that—try to get fingerprints? What good would that do?*

Lisa and Brandon were waiting at the dock, so Sherlock and I surrendered the wave runners to them. Lisa gave Sherlock a funny look when he opened the seat on his machine and removed the soft-drink can. "Trash," he said in answer to her unspoken question. She nodded and climbed aboard the wave runner. I don't think she noticed the careful way the young detective was handling the "trash."

Lisa and Brandon went roaring across the lake, and Sherlock turned to me. "Let's go to the cabin," he told me. "I want to dust this for fingerprints."

I fell in step beside him. "Fingerprints!" I echoed. "You brought your fingerprint kit up here?"

"Of course."

"You think that can belonged to the fisherman, don't you?" I asked.

He nodded. "Of course."

"How can you be so sure?"

"The can was lying on its side with soda pop trickling out," Sherlock replied, "and the can was still cold. Judging from the amount of soda on the ground and the rate at which it was pouring out, I figure that the can had been on the ground for less than thirty seconds. There was no one else around, so it must have belonged to him."

I shrugged. "OK, so it *was* his. Why do you want his fingerprints?"

"When we find out who he is," Sherlock told me, "then perhaps we can determine what he was up to."

"Something mighty strange is going on here at Thunderbird Lake," I said. An idea suddenly occurred to me, and I grabbed Sherlock's arm. "Do you think that this man could be connected with the mysterious plane that came in last night? That was mighty strange, too, you know."

Sherlock shook his head. "Penny," he said, "I'm not going to form an opinion until I have more of the facts."

"But take a guess," I coaxed. "Don't you think it's a possibility?"

"I'm not even going to venture a guess," he insisted. "To do so might influence my thinking and lead me to a faulty conclusion. I simply need to wait until we know more."

I stared at him. *Not even venture a guess as to what's going on? This guy's thought processes sure operate differently than mine!*

"Wait here," Sherlock told me as he set the soft drink can carefully on a table. "Watch the can for me. I'll bring the fingerprint kit out on the deck." I sat down at the patio table to wait, and he reappeared in less than a minute. He was wearing rubber gloves and carrying a small cardboard box. He took out a small soft-bristled brush and a bottle of white powder, and then began to meticulously dust the soft drink can with the powder.

I watched in silence until I couldn't stand it any longer. I had to ask. "Any good prints?"

Sherlock groaned and shook his head. "There are several prints," he said, disappointed, "but they're all smeared. None are clear enough to be worth anything." He set the can on the table and gave it a look of disgust. "The aluminum skin of the can should have been an excellent surface for retaining usable prints."

Robert served pizza for lunch. We met Mr. Diamond on the deck at 12:30, and Robert and Maimee appeared with two huge, steaming hot pizzas, one mushroom and one pepperoni. I eyed the mushroom pizza hungrily as Robert set it on the table in front of us. It was so hot that the cheese was still bubbling and blowing little puffs of steam. My favorite pizza comes from Pizza Shack, and I've never cared much for the homemade variety, but this looked good! (As it turned out, Robert's pizza was better than Pizza Shack's.)

We had prayer, and then Robert served me a huge slice of the mushroom pizza. "Looks good," I teased the little caretaker, "but I wonder how many fat grams it has."

Robert snorted. "Fat grams?" he grated in that buzz saw voice of his. "Why are young people always worried about fat grams? When I was your age, 'fat grams' meant overweight grandmothers!"

I laughed and bit into the pizza. I burned my mouth, but was it good! If Robert keeps making them like this, he'll put Pizza Shack out of business. For dessert, he served us a fruit pizza that Maimee had made. It was delicious, with a sweet pastry-type crust, sweet cream cheese filling, and a layer of fresh strawberries, peaches, and blueberries on top. The fruit was arranged in concentric rings around a huge strawberry in the center, which gave the whole dessert the appearance of an archery target.

We spent the rest of the afternoon goofing around, talking, riding the wave runners, and just enjoying our unexpected time off from school. I finally remembered to call home and tell my mom that we had reached the lake all right, and that everything was fine. I didn't mention the mystery plane or the mystery man.

As I hung up the phone, it rang, so I answered it. "Diamonds."

"This is Tina Lewis," a familiar voice told me. "Melissa's going to be just fine. She's awake and talking and eating, and the doctors say she's going to be fine." The woman began to cry. "I just wanted to tell your friend thank you for saving my little girl's life. Tell him that Melissa's all right, and that the doctors say she can go home tomorrow."

"I'll tell him, Mrs. Lewis," I said. "We're thankful that she's OK."

"Well, thanks for everything. I've got to get back to Melissa. Come over and see us some time."

My eyes were misty as I hung up the phone. "Thank you, Lord," I prayed softly, "for giving Sherlock such an incredible mind!"

"How about a little fishing?" Mr. Diamond asked after supper that night. "I know a place where the fish stand in line for a chance at your bait. If you don't put a line in the water quick enough, they'll actually jump into the boat to get at it!"

"Daddy has a favorite fishing spot on the north wing," Lisa told us. "The fish may not be quite as eager as he makes them out to be, but the fishing *is* good. You'll love it!"

"I'm game," Brandon said. "Let me at them."

I looked at Robert. "Will you go with us?"

The little man shook his head. "Put me in a canoe, and I'll be just fine. But you won't catch me more than fifty feet from shore in a powerboat. I don't trust them." He grinned suddenly. "You'll have to go after those fish without my help. But I'll tell you what—you catch 'em, and I'll fry 'em. How's that for a deal?" He walked toward the cabin with an armload of dishes.

"Robert was out in the Atlantic on a fishing boat when the engine quit," Mr. Diamond told us in a low voice. "The boat drifted out to sea and was lost for several days. Robert and his friends nearly died. That was thirty years ago, but he hasn't gone out on a powerboat since."

"How long has he worked for you?" Sherlock asked.

"A little over six years," Mr. Diamond replied. "I hired him just after Diamond Point was built. He was an alcoholic and had lost his family as a result, but he accepted the Lord as his Savior less than six months after he started working here. He's had complete victory over the bottle, and his wife has come back to him. Now he's one of my most trusted employees. You won't find a more loyal man than Robert Biddler."

He looked up as Robert came back outside. "Is the *Gemstone* fueled?"

The caretaker nodded. "She's ready to go. I'll get you some soft drinks for the cooler, and you just need to remember to check your tackle."

The moon was just rising over Eagle's Nest as the *Gemstone* cruised slowly out from the boathouse. "Leave the running lights off, Daddy," Lisa requested, "so that we can watch the stars."

Mr. Diamond laughed. "Just don't let me run into something in the dark then." He pushed the throttle down a notch or two, and the bow of the boat lifted gently. I would guess that we were doing about ten or twelve miles an hour.

"Penny and I will watch," Lisa replied.

The *Gemstone* was a bowrider, which means that it had a space for passengers in front of the windshield. Lisa and I were sitting up front, while Sherlock and Brandon were back with Mr. Diamond. I leaned back on the cushions and looked at the sky. The moon hung over the lake like a huge silver dollar that had somehow been suspended in the sky. The stars glittered like diamonds. An owl hooted somewhere in the distance, and the lonely sound echoed across the water. It was a beautiful night.

"Look at the senator's place," Brandon remarked. "Tonight must be party night!"

We all looked up. Briarwood was lit up so bright you would have thought that they were celebrating the hundredth anniversary of the invention of the light bulb. The mansion was ablaze with lights. The yard was brilliantly lit with huge floodlights that reflected off the white stone of the building with such a glare that it almost hurt your eyes from a quarter of a mile away. The steep driveway was lined with parked cars, and we could see long fancy limousines pulling up into the circular drive at the side of the mansion. On the north side of the mansion, several dozen guests in formal clothes were dancing on the huge deck overlooking the lake. They even had a small orchestra!

"The senator must be entertaining some important dignitaries," Lisa remarked. "Look at those cars."

We all stared at Senator Greene's mansion as the *Gemstone* cruised quietly past. They were having quite a party! The music from the orchestra wafted softly across the lake, creating a most unusual atmosphere for a fishing trip.

Mr. Diamond guided the *Gemstone* to a spot in the middle of the lake just south of the channel where we had seen the fearful fisherman. I estimated that we were about a mile and a half north of Briarwood. We couldn't see the mansion because of the woods along the shoreline, but above the trees we could actually see the glow of the lights against the darkness of the sky. "This is it," Mr. Diamond said, shutting off the motor and dropping a small anchor overboard. "Get ready for some action! Once the fish find out we're here, they'll be fighting each other for the privilege of being the first one on the hook."

He reached for the switch that turns on the marker lights, but Lisa caught his hand. "Can we leave it off, Daddy? There's enough moonlight to fish by, and it's more fun this way. We can turn the lights on if another boat comes out our way, which isn't likely."

Mr. Diamond shrugged. "Sure, honey." He stooped and opened a long storage compartment in the floor of the boat. "OK, everybody, let's get our tackle ready. I'll pass out the fishing rods, but we have to do it in the dark. My persistent daughter doesn't want any lights."

It took a few minutes to sort out the fishing tackle by moonlight, but in a short while we were each in possession of a rod and reel. To my surprise, Lisa was the one who passed out the worms. She even helped me put mine on the hook. She's not your average millionaire's daughter.

Sherlock had his line in the water before anyone else was even ready. Just like Mr. Diamond had promised, he had a strike almost immediately. It seemed that the fish must have grabbed the bait before it even hit the water. "I got one!" he exclaimed. "It feels like a big one."

"Hang onto him," Mr. Diamond answered. "Everyone keep your lines out of the water until Sherlock brings him in," he said, addressing the rest of us. "No sense in getting our lines tangled this early in the game. There'll be plenty of time for that later."

Sherlock fought the fish for several minutes while the rest of us waited breathlessly to see what he had. The fish ran under the boat several times, trying to snag the line. He even jumped into the air two or three times in an effort to shake the hook, but Sherlock stayed right with him. Finally, he was able to draw the fish alongside the boat so that Mr. Diamond could get him in the landing net.

"Sherlock, you got a beauty!" the millionaire said as he lifted the struggling fish from the water. "He's a good four pounds, at least!"

Sherlock's grin was visible even in the darkness. "It's my first fish!" he whispered ecstatically to me. "I've never been fishing before!"

"Beginner's luck," I hissed at him. "You probably won't catch another all night!"

Mr. Diamond grabbed the fish by the lower lip and lifted him from the net for us to see. "Large mouth bass," he told us. "This is trophy size!" He opened the lid on a special, water-filled compartment called a live well and dropped the bass in. "Nice catch, Sherlock!"

We fished for the next three hours. Just as Mr. Diamond had promised, the fish were hungry, and time after time they volunteered for hook duty. The *Gemstone* was a beehive of activity as one person after another reeled in fish after fish. It seemed like we were playing musical chairs in the boat, stepping out of the way of the person who was landing the next fish, watching as the fish was taken off the hook and stowed in the live well, and then standing clear as the lucky fisherman re-baited the hook and made another cast. In less than an hour, the live well in the stern was full, and Mr. Diamond started using the one in the bow where Lisa and I were.

There was only one problem—I wasn't catching a thing! Mr. Diamond, Lisa, Brandon and Sherlock were all having a ball, reeling in the fish almost as fast as they could throw their lines in the water. But for some strange reason, I wasn't catching a single fish! I'd bait my hook, toss the line in the water, and give a little jerk when I felt a tug on the line. But when I'd pull in the line, all that I'd have would be an empty hook. The fish were stealing my bait. Everyone else in the boat was catching fish, but I was just passing out free worms. It was pretty frustrating.

I pushed the light button on my watch and glanced at the time. 11:30. We had been on the water for over three hours, and I still hadn't caught anything! *Come on, Penny,* I told myself, *you can do better than this! If they can catch fish, so can you.*

I stepped to the bow of the boat and drew back my rod, ready to cast the line as far as I could. As I leaned back, I happened to glance upward and, to my surprise, spotted red and white marker lights high overhead. The phantom airplane had returned!

"Look," I whispered, so excited that I could barely get the words out, "the airplane from last night! See him? He's coming in from the north." Just then, the purr of the aircraft's engines drifted down to us.

We forgot all about fishing. All five of us stood open-mouthed in the boat, fishing rods in hand, and watched the plane circle the lake. It descended rapidly. And then, just as it had done the night before, the aircraft began blinking its lights.

"Look," Sherlock whispered. "On the shore."

I glanced over in the direction that Sherlock was pointing. To my astonishment, I saw a light flashing on and off. Someone on the west side of the lake was signaling the plane. The light blinked three times, stayed off for a couple of seconds, blinked five times, and then blinked once. The light stopped flashing and I glanced up at the plane. The pilot was blinking the plane's lights. He and the person on the ground were definitely signaling each other!

And then, the lights on the plane just simply winked out. I watched for about fifteen seconds, but they didn't come back on. We could hear faintly the plane's engines, though, so we knew that it was still there. It sounded like he was circling the lake. But why was he doing it with his lights off? I watched the place on shore where the light had been flashing, but there were no more signals. Just darkness.

I scooted over beside Sherlock, who was writing numerals on the back of his own hand. I couldn't see very well in the darkness, but I would have known without looking that he was using a pen with green ink. "What in the world is going on?" I whispered.

"Keep quiet," he whispered softly. "Just watch."

The aircraft circled in the darkness for three or four more minutes. I was expecting it to come down and land on the lake like it did the night before, but apparently, the pilot had other plans. He just kept circling and circling. I was getting a crick in my neck from watching.

I studied the shoreline, trying to see the area where the signals had originated. The moon was fairly bright, but I couldn't see a thing. It was just too dark.

"Look at that," Sherlock breathed softly. His voice had a note of excitement like I had never heard before.

I looked upwards and suddenly I saw why. I stared, hardly able to believe what I was seeing.

SIX

MAX AND NORM

The mysterious plane was still circling overhead, just as it had been for the past several minutes. But what had caught Sherlock's attention were two white lights that were slowly drifting down toward the lake. They had shot out from the side of the plane and dropped from the sky, falling fast like shooting stars. But then they slowed down and just seemed to hang in the air like ordinary stars.

"Parachutes," Sherlock whispered. "They're using parachutes!"

"Don't be ridiculous," I whispered back. "Why would anyone parachute in here at night?"

"I didn't say that they were people," he retorted. "They're probably cargo chutes."

Brandon slid over beside us. "Hey, Sherlock," he whispered, "what's going on here? This is weird!"

The five of us sat quietly watching the tiny lights drift silently toward the lake. For a while it seemed that the lights weren't even moving; they just seemed to hang there in the sky above the water. I would guess that we watched them for a good three minutes. All of a sudden, a boat motor roared to life over by the shore and a tiny white light went bouncing across the water toward the spot where the lights were going to land! Whoever was driving the boat had to be the same person that had been signaling the plane, and now he was going to retrieve whatever it was that the plane had dropped.

"Daddy, let's get out of here," Lisa suggested in a trembling voice. "I don't like the looks of this!"

"I think we're OK," her father answered quietly. "They don't even know that we're here. And the *Gemstone* will outrun anything on this lake if it has to."

The falling lights had reached the surface of the lake by this time, and we could no longer see them. But we could still see the tiny light on the boat. It stopped out in the middle of the lake, less than two hundred yards from where the *Gemstone* rocked gently in the darkness. After a moment or two, the engine on the boat revved up, and the light went bouncing across the lake again, only to stop again after a few seconds. The light stayed in one place for two or three minutes and then went bobbing across the water to the accompaniment of the roaring motor.

We watched in silence as the light disappeared around the bend to vanish somewhere on the south wing of the Thunderbird. Mr. Diamond started the *Gemstone's* engine. "Well, it's getting late," he said. "I guess we'd better head back."

"They got what they came for," Sherlock said, referring to the people in the mysterious boat. "I'd give up pizza for a year to find out what came down on those parachutes." Knowing Sherlock like I do, I realized that it wouldn't be long before he'd figure out a way to do just that. But I had no idea just how much danger we would get ourselves into when it happened.

Wednesday morning marked the beginning of our third day at Thunderbird Lake. I thought about it as we finished another of Robert's fabulous breakfasts. The plan was to stay at the lake until early Saturday afternoon and then head for home. I sighed, not even wanting to think about going home yet. We were having so much fun, but we only had a little over three days left. And what if that wasn't enough time to figure out what the phantom airplane was up to? Were we just supposed to walk away from an unsolved mystery?

"Thanks for breakfast, Robert," Sherlock said, as he reached for his sixth or seventh blueberry pancake. (For a little guy, he eats a LOT!) "This was another super meal. You're fantastic!"

The little caretaker beamed. "Glad you liked it, son," he rasped. "It's fun to cook for people who appreciate it."

The phone rang just then, and Mr. Diamond answered it. He listened for several seconds and then said, "Certainly, Mrs. Pendergrass. She's right here." He handed the phone to Lisa. "It's for you."

"Good morning, Mrs. Pendergrass," Lisa said, as she took the phone. She listened for a minute or two and then said, "Sure! We'll be glad to go. What is—oh, OK. No problem. We're just finishing breakfast, so we'll leave here in five minutes. No, we're glad to do it for you. We'll see you in just a little bit."

She hung up the phone and took her seat at the table. "Mrs. Pendergrass wants us to run down to Aysee's for her. Her car has a broken fan belt, so she can't drive in herself."

"What does she want us to get for her?" Brandon asked.

"A fan belt," Lisa replied. "That's why we're going to Aysee's."

Brandon frowned. "Who'll put it on for her? I'd be willing to, but I wouldn't even know how."

Lisa laughed. "She'll do it herself."

"Mrs. Pendergrass?" Brandon was shocked. "By herself? She's over eighty years old!"

Lisa laughed again. "You don't know Mrs. Pendergrass." She jumped up from the table. "Daddy, may we take the scooters?"

Mr. Diamond nodded. "Of course."

Brandon, Sherlock, and I followed Lisa out to the huge eight-car garage. Lisa punched several digits into the keypad beside the first garage door, and the door opened silently. We saw six blue motor scooters parked in a neat row against the left wall. "Choose one," she told us. "They're all identical. The keys are in the ignitions."

We each hopped on a scooter and raised the kickstands. Lisa showed us how to start the engines and put the vehicles in gear. After a quick lesson on starting and stopping, we followed her from the garage. Lisa rode her scooter close to the garage and pushed a button to close the door.

"Will these things make it up that trail?" I asked.

Lisa nodded. "Daddy had them all re-geared," she replied. "They'll climb almost anywhere."

"Where are we going?" Brandon asked. "I thought we were miles from civilization."

"The little town of Comanche is just over two miles from here," Lisa answered. "It's about eight miles by car, but we'll take the forest trail, which is much shorter." She grinned. "If you think Willoughby is small, wait until you see Comanche."

"Why is it called Comanche?" Sherlock asked, twisting the throttle grip on his scooter and revving the little engine. "The Comanches never lived in this part of the country; they were plains Indians. And they didn't call themselves Comanches— that was the white man's name for them. They called themselves 'Nemena,' which meant 'the true people.' "

Lisa shrugged. "I guess I've never wondered about it. Ready? Let's go." She released the brake and drove from the yard with the rest of us following.

We went buzzing up a narrow trail that wound its way through the woods behind Diamond Point. The fall leaves must have been at their peak that day, and the forest was alive with vivid, vibrant color. Fiery red maples, golden tamarack and birch, orange sugar maples, purple ash, and butter-yellow hickories all contrasted against the deep blue and green of the spruce and pines. A light breeze stirred in the treetops, causing the trees to moan and whisper to each other like senior citizens at a Sunday school picnic. The woods seemed alive. I've never seen a prettier fall day.

My scooter whined like an oversized mosquito, but it climbed like an energetic mountain goat. At one point, the trail skirted the edge of a clearing, and we could see Mrs. Pendergrass's farm down below. After ten or fifteen minutes of buzzing up steep hills and flying down the other side at breakneck speeds, the trail dumped us out of the woods, and we found ourselves in a sleepy little town perched on the side of a hill.

We followed Lisa's scooter to the front of a ramshackle cinderblock building with a Plexiglas sign reading "Aysee Brothers Hardware." Parking the scooters on the narrow sidewalk, we walked past a huge plate glass window with a display of chain saws and snow blowers. When we opened the door, a little brass bell at the top of the door announced our arrival.

To my surprise, the interior of the store was immaculate. The building was old, but the freshly painted walls and the mirror finish on the hardwood floor gave evidence that someone still cared. The well-stocked shelves were neat, orderly, and clean.

Brandon disappeared down one of the narrow aisles, but Sherlock and I followed Lisa to a service counter at one side of the store. A thin, gray-haired man with a yellow pencil tucked behind his right ear stepped out of the back room. "Lisa Diamond!" he exclaimed. "What a surprise to see ya! What are ya doin' up here?"

"Mr. Aysee," Lisa said, "I'd like you to meet some friends of mine, Sherlock Jones and Penny Gordon. I go to school with them. We're spending the week at Diamond Point with Daddy." The look in her eyes and the tone of her voice told me immediately that Lisa considered this man a good friend.

"Pleased to meet ya," the man said, extending a thin hand to shake hands with me and then Sherlock. "I'm Norman Aysee, part-owner of this humble establishment. If you're friends of Lisa Diamond's, you're friends of mine." The phone rang in the back room just then, and the man hurried toward the sound. "Be right back," he called over his shoulder.

Ten seconds later, he stepped back through the doorway. "Lisa Diamond!" he said, his eyes lighting up with delight. "What a surprise! What are ya doin' here?"

I was puzzled. Was this man so old that his memory was completely gone? He had been gone only a few seconds, but already he had forgotten that he had just seen Lisa. *Maybe he has Alzheimer's disease,* I told myself. I looked at Sherlock, but he had a polite, friendly smile on his face as if nothing was wrong.

"Mr. Aysee," Lisa said, "I'd like you to meet some friends of mine, Sherlock Jones and Penny Gordon. We go to school together. We're spending the week at Diamond Point with Daddy." She introduced us just as she had thirty seconds ago, but she acted like nothing was wrong and that it was perfectly natural to give your friends a double introduction.

"Pleased to meet ya," the man said, shaking hands with us just as he had thirty seconds before. "I'm Maxwell Aysee, part-owner of this humble establishment. If you're friends of Lisa Diamond's, you're friends of mine."

I smiled politely. This man might be a friend of Lisa's, but he was weird!

And then, to my astonishment, the man stepped from the back room again and stood beside himself at the counter! There were two of these guys! They both had the same face and voice, the same green flannel shirt, the yellow pencil behind the right ear, everything. Suddenly I realized—they were identical twins!

The Aysee brothers laughed at my reaction. "Thought ya were seein' double, didn't ya?" they said in unison.

Lisa laughed merrily. "These men are twins, Penny," she said. "Max and Norm Aysee. But I can't tell you which is which. Nobody can!" She looked at the men, and then back at me. "The only way I can tell them apart is if I see one of them write. Max is right-handed, and Norm is left-handed. Other than that, they're identical. They dress alike, talk alike, and even think alike!"

Sherlock looked from one man to another. "If you're identical, why is one of you left-handed and the other right-handed?"

Both men opened their mouths to answer, and then Norm paused and gestured for Max to proceed. "Ma didn't like the idea of us being left-handed," Max said, "so she tried to make me write with my right hand. She succeeded, but when she saw how much grief she had caused me, she let Norm alone. Other than when I write, I'm as left-handed as Norm."

Norm spoke up. "We've had a lot of fun being identical twins. Even our own mother couldn't tell us apart."

Sherlock studied both men for a few seconds and then announced, "I can."

The Aysee twins laughed at him. "I don't think so, son," they chorused together.

"Try me," Sherlock insisted. "You're Max, right?" he said, pointing at one twin. The man nodded. "So you're Norm." Sherlock pointed to the other man, who nodded in agreement. "All right," Sherlock said again. "Try me. Would you both step into the back room, and then come back out? I'll tell you which is which."

Max and Norm looked at each other in amusement. "If he can do it, he'll be the first," Max said.

"Just what I was thinking," Norm agreed.

The brothers walked into the back room, waited a few seconds and then returned. "You're Max," Sherlock said, pointing to one man, "and you're Norm." He pointed to the other.

The men looked at each other and grinned. "He's right," they both said.

"Big deal!" I groaned. "You had a fifty-fifty chance of being right. You got lucky."

"I can do it ten times in a row," Sherlock replied. "Watch. Gentlemen?"

Max and Norm walked into the back room and returned. Again, Sherlock identified them correctly. *They're just playing along with him,* I realized. *No matter which name he calls them by, they agree with him, so it looks like he's right. I'll fix him!*

"Sherlock, turn your back and close your eyes," I ordered. "Lisa, watch him to be sure he doesn't cheat." When Sherlock's back was turned, I had the men switch places so Max was now on the right and Norm on the left. When Sherlock turned around, he identified the men correctly. I repeated the maneuver half a dozen times, sometimes having the men switch, other times just having them move their feet so that it sounded like they were switching. But Sherlock never missed.

"OK," I said finally, "how are you doing it? How can you tell which is which?"

Sherlock just grinned at me. "You're seeing what I'm seeing, Penny. Figure it out."

I studied the men's hands and faces and then their clothes, trying to find some identifying mark. A mole, a grease spot on a shirt, anything. But there was nothing. "I can't, Sherlock! You know I can't. Now, tell me!"

He just shook his head. "Think it through, Penny."

I was frustrated. I knew that Sherlock had noticed something about the elderly twins that I hadn't, but I had no idea what it was. I also knew that Sherlock wasn't going to tell me until he was good and ready, and that bugged me.

Brandon came walking up to the counter just then. He stared at the Aysee brothers for several seconds and then blurted, "Incredible! Clones!"

"And this," Lisa said, "is Brandon Marshall." She pulled several comic book-type tracts from her shirt pocket and laid them on the counter. "I have some more booklets," she told the men. "See if there are any new ones."

The Aysee brothers stepped close to the counter and stood shoulder to shoulder. Max—I think it was Max on the right—reached out and picked up the top tract. "We've read this one, Miss Lisa." He set it to one side. Norm reached out for the next tract. "This is a new one. We'll read it." He set it beside the stack.

Max reached out and picked up the next booklet. "This is a new one." He set it beside the stack. Norm took the next one. "We've read this one." He set it to the side.

They went through the whole stack of ten or twelve tracts that way, working together and taking turns looking through the tracts. They worked together as one person—a two-headed, four-armed person. It was uncanny the way they thought and moved together, with one brother's actions complementing the other's.

They ended up with six new tracts. "Thanks, Miss Lisa," they said in unison. "We'll read these tonight." Max pocketed three of the tracts, and Norm pocketed the other three. "Now, what was it," Max began, but Norm finished the question, "that you came in for?"

"We need an alternator belt for a Ford," Lisa replied. She told him the year and model.

"505K6," Max told his brother. "You get it, and I'll ring it up."

Norm stepped out from behind the counter. "It's $13.48," he said to Max, who rang it up on the register.

Sherlock looked around. "You carry auto parts?" he asked. "In a hardware store?"

The old man seemed amused by the question. "It's a small town, son," he replied. "I guess we carry a little of everything."

Lisa paid for her purchase and headed for the door with the fan belt. "Read the tracts," she called. "I'll check back with you."

"We will, Miss Lisa," the brothers said in unison. "It's a delight to see you again!"

"They acted like they were really glad to see you," I remarked to Lisa as we started up the motor scooters. "And you acted as if they were really good friends."

"They are," she replied. "They live side-by-side in two little houses on the north wing of the Thunderbird, the two little places just north of Mrs. Lewis's property. Neither man has ever married. Norm saved me from drowning the first summer we were at Diamond Point. I guess I was only six or seven. He and his brother have been like grandfathers to me ever since." She sighed. "I sure wish I could lead them to the Lord. They're both good men, but they really don't see their need for Jesus. I've been praying for them for the last five years."

I thought about her words as our scooters buzzed back through the forest trail. The thing that I admire most about Lisa is not her beauty, her money, or her sweet personality. She loves the Lord with all her heart, and she has a burden for lost souls. She wants the Lord to use her, but I've noticed that she's not afraid to give a tract to adults, or even witness to them. I'd like to be more like her.

We left the scooters at Diamond Point and walked to Mrs. Pendergrass's farm with the alternator belt. When we reached the farm, we found her down by the barn under the hood of a car that was older than any of us. She was standing on a cinderblock to be able to reach her work. It's hard to believe that this woman is over eighty years old!

She heard us coming and ducked out from under the hood. She had a ratchet in her hand (I asked Sherlock later what it was called, just so I'd be able to name it correctly) and a smear of grease on her face, but her dress was perfectly clean. "Just loosening up the alternator so I can put the new belt on," she told us, wiping her forehead with the back of her hand. "Mercy, those bolts were rusted tight."

"Can we help?" Brandon offered, towering over her.

Mrs. Pendergrass shook her head. "I've got it now, Brandon. All I need to do is put the new belt on."

I felt a sharp object stab me in the back of the leg, behind my knee. I whirled around. One of Mrs. Pendergrass's big red chickens had sneaked up and attacked me from behind!

Brandon stepped around the side of the car and suddenly noticed two aluminum canoes lying against the side of the barn. "Canoes! Mrs. Pendergrass, do you think we could—uh, would you let us, uh . . ."

"Borrow them?" the old lady finished with a chuckle. "I suppose so. They belonged to a troop of Boy Scouts that used to come camping on my property. Haven't seen those boys in fifteen years. I suppose the scouts don't even remember that those old canoes are still here. Just promise me that you'll take care of them."

I walked over and squatted beside the canoes. "These could really be a lot of fun, couldn't they? Do you have any paddles?"

Mrs. Pendergrass pulled the alternator belt from the package. "They're in the barn, Penny. You'll find them leaning against the wall beside the tack rack."

If I had had any idea what Sherlock would use the canoes for the next night and what would happen as a result, I suppose I would have run away from those canoes as fast as I could go.

SEVEN

ANOTHER FISHING TRIP

"The Little Bear empties into Thunderbird Lake," Mrs. Pendergrass told us as she leaned over the grill of her old car to install the new alternator belt. "Why don't you take the canoes down the river and paddle over to Diamond Point? You can use the canoes for the next few days if you like, or simply bring them back if you decide that canoeing isn't for you."

We carried the canoes through the soybean field and launched them in the river. The two boys got into one canoe, Brandon in the stern and Sherlock in the bow, while Lisa got into the stern of the second canoe, leaving me the seat in the bow. Paddles in hand, we shoved out into the lazy current. This was going to be fun!

We quickly found out that canoeing isn't as easy as it looks. Lisa and I are both right-handed, so I suppose that's why we both started paddling on the right side. Our canoe began turning to the left, but I didn't know what to do about it.

"Switch sides!" Lisa shouted at me. "Paddle on the other side!"

While I was trying to figure out how to do that, the canoe rammed the bank on the far side of the river. The bow stuck fast in the mud, and the current slowly swung the stern around until it was facing downstream. At that point the front end pulled free of the bank and the canoe continued on down the river. We were going backwards!

I looked over at Brandon and Sherlock, but they weren't faring much better. Their canoe was cutting sharply to the left and Brandon was shouting, "Switch sides!" He and Sherlock started paddling on the left, and the canoe started swinging to the right. By the time they switched again, the canoe had drifted too far to the right, and they were out of control again. Struggling to get the canoe straight, they again overcorrected and went too far to the left. They were zigzagging like a PT boat trying to avoid torpedoes! Lisa and I laughed until our sides hurt.

We felt a sudden thump from behind and turned around. Our canoe was still floating backwards, and we had drifted right smack into a huge rock in the middle of the stream. Lisa leaned out to push our canoe away from the rock, and the canoe leaned with her.

"You're tipping us!" I screamed. I leaned in the opposite direction to counterbalance her weight. "Lisa! You're tipping us!" She lunged the other way just as I leaned, and we nearly tipped over to the right.

Needless to say, our little canoe trip was not that much fun. Fortunately, Diamond Point was not far away. But by the time we got there, we had all decided that canoeing wasn't for us. "We'll take the canoes back to Mrs. Pendergrass after lunch," I declared as we climbed out of the treacherous craft at the dock, "and tell her thanks, but no thanks. These things are dangerous!"

Robert was painting the side of the boathouse, and he overheard my remark. "Nonsense," he growled. "A canoe is the safest watercraft in the world when it's handled right."

"And the most dangerous when it's handled wrong," I retorted. "That's what we were doing."

"Everyone take a seat on the edge of the dock," Robert ordered. "It's time for your first lesson in canoeing."

"I'd rather ride the wave runners," I declared.

The little caretaker snorted. "Sit down and listen up, Penny." He grinned at me and disappeared inside the boathouse. Moments later he stepped back out with five life vests, which he tossed into the canoes. "The first rule in canoeing is this: never get into the canoe without your life vest. The law doesn't say that you have to wear it, but it does say that you have to have it in the boat. One for each person. The safest way, of course, is to go ahead and wear the things."

Robert tied the first canoe to one of the dock pilings and then climbed into the second canoe and knelt just forward of the stern seat. He picked up a paddle. "Here's how to hold your paddle," he told us, "upper hand over the end of the grip, lower hand gripping the shaft just above the blade." He demonstrated the proper grip for us.

"Now this is called a J stroke. It keeps the canoe from turning away from your paddle." I quickly realized that Robert was an expert with a canoe. In the next few minutes he showed us how to make that little boat go exactly where we wanted it. In addition to teaching us the J stroke, he taught us other paddle movements such as the draw, the sweep, and the back sweep. He even showed us how to use a maneuver called a low brace to recover a tipping canoe.

"Once you know what you're doing, the canoe is the safest type of boat in the world," he told us. "Watch this." He stood up in the center of the canoe, planted his feet wide, and then began to shift his weight from side to side. It almost looked like he was dancing some strange sort of jig. The canoe rocked back and forth so violently that the gunwales nearly touched the water. I expected the canoe to tip over at any moment. After fifteen seconds or so, Robert sat back down, and the canoe stopped rocking.

"Believe it or not, I was in perfect control of this canoe the entire time," he said, picking up his paddle. "When you get your balance and get the feel for the canoe, you can make these little boats do almost anything. A canoe is the most graceful water-craft ever designed."

He paddled straight toward the center of the lake with long, smooth strokes of the paddle. The canoe knifed through the water like a porpoise. Thirty yards from the dock, Robert did two quick back sweeps with the paddle and the bow swung around to point straight at the dock. Paddling hard, he raced the canoe straight for us. When the bow of the canoe was less than four feet from the dock he did a hard back sweep, swinging the bow quickly to the left. The canoe glided to a stop parallel to the dock with the gunwale of the canoe less than two inches from the edge! Robert grinned up at us. "A canoe will do exactly what you tell it to."

He stood up, leaned forward and grasped the gunwale on each side of the canoe, and then carefully walked forward. When he was in the center, he sat down again. "OK, everyone in the canoes," he ordered. "We'll head back over to the Little Bear and find out how well you listened."

After lunch Sherlock and I took two of the scooters and buzzed into Comanche. I wasn't sure what we were after, but I followed Sherlock inside the Aysee Brother's Hardware. One of the twins met us at the counter. "Howdy, Sherlock, Penny," he greeted us. "How's your day going?"

"Fine, Mr. Aysee," I replied. I turned to Sherlock. "OK, which one is this? Max or Norm?"

"Max," Sherlock replied without hesitation.

I looked at Mr. Aysee. "Is he right?"

The man grinned. "He hasn't missed yet."

"I need a high-powered spotlight," Sherlock told Max. "The kind that runs off the cigarette lighter in a car. But I need a bright one."

"We've got just the thing you need," Max told us, leading us to the second aisle from the end. He picked up a cardboard box. "Two million candlepower. This thing will shine from one end of the Thunderbird to the other."

I was impressed. "Really?"

Max laughed. "Well, almost. I was pulling your leg. But it is one powerful spotlight."

Sherlock was examining the box. "Just what we need," he declared. "How much?"

"Nineteen ninety-five. That'll come to just over twenty-one dollars with the tax."

A look of disappointment swept over Sherlock's face. "I only have fourteen dollars," he told Max. "Do you have anything cheaper?"

"Just a regular flashlight."

Sherlock shook his head. "That won't do for what I need." He thought for a moment and then asked, "Would you be willing to rent this to me?"

Max looked puzzled. "Rent it?"

"Sure!" Sherlock replied. "I'll pay you ten dollars to use it until Saturday morning and return it, with the box, in perfect condition. Please?"

Max thought it over. "All right," he said finally, "but just because you're a friend of Lisa's." Sherlock handed him a ten-dollar bill.

"So what do you need the searchlight for?" I asked as we headed for the scooters. "Why did you pay that much to rent it when you could have *bought* a good flashlight for less than that?"

Sherlock flashed me his trademark I'm-not-going-to-tell-you-right-now grin. "I need it the next time we go fishing," he replied. "You'll see." He started the motor scooter.

"How did you know that was Max?" I shouted at him above the noise of the engine. He just grinned at me and pulled away from the store. I started my scooter and hurried to catch up.

That night we were driving back from church when Mr. Diamond pulled over to the guardrail overlooking the lake. "It's a beautiful night," he told us. "Anyone interested in some night fishing? The fish are waiting!"

"Count me out," I sighed. "Last night was rather frustrating. I didn't catch a thing!"

"I looked at your rod and reel today," the millionaire told me, "and I think I discovered your problem. The barb was missing from your hook. It was sheared clean off! You were fishing with three quarters of a hook."

"I only had part of a hook?"

"The tip was missing," he repeated, "so there was nothing to hold the fish. It's no wonder you couldn't catch anything!"

I looked quizzically at Lisa. "How come you didn't notice that?" I asked. "You helped me bait my hook the first time."

She shrugged. "I guess it was too dark, and I couldn't see it. I'm sorry."

"Mr. Diamond," I asked, "how could that have happened? Would the hook just break?"

"I don't think so," he replied, guiding the van through a tight curve. "It looked like it had been cut."

"Cut?" I echoed. "Why would anyone do that?" I heard a snicker from the back seat and looked back to see Brandon struggling to keep a straight face. "OK, Mr. Marshall," I demanded, "what do you know about this?"

He grinned. "There was a pair of pliers in the tackle box, and you weren't looking, so . . ."

Suddenly I was so angry that I was almost crying. "Why would you do that?" I shrilled at him. "You ruined a whole night's fishing for me! Do you know how frustrated I was? Everyone else was catching fish, and I was the only one in the boat who wasn't catching anything!" I gave an angry snort. "If I had known last night that you did that, I would have thrown you overboard!"

"Penny, Penny," Robert said softly, "calm down."

I was still angry with Brandon. "How could you do such a thing?"

He looked at me impishly. "Remember last year when you told Mr. Murphy that I was the one who trapped all the teachers in the ladies' bathroom? And I said that I'd get even?" He leaned forward. "Guess what? We're even!"

"Oh, no, we're not," I huffed. "Wait till tonight. Wait till you have a nice six-pounder on the line. I'll cut your line!"

"We're even," Brandon insisted.

"Oh, no, we're not! I'm going to—"

"Penny," Mr. Diamond interrupted quietly, "That's enough."

We reached Diamond Point just then, and he swung the van into the driveway. "Let's change clothes," he said, "and meet at the dock in ten minutes. Robert, could you find some kind of a snack item for us?"

The moon was busily scurrying from one dark cloud to another as Lisa and I headed down to the boathouse. Robert already had the *Gemstone* idling at the end of the dock. "Coming with us?" I teased.

"Only if you're going in a canoe," he replied jokingly.

Mr. Diamond and the boys came rushing down just then. We all scrambled aboard and cruised off across the moonlit lake. For some reason, Mr. Diamond left the running lights off. We cruised to a point just north of the body of the Thunderbird, shut down the engine, and threw the anchor overboard. I looked up to notice that we were just over a quarter of a mile from Briarwood. The mansion was dark with just three or four interior lights on. I thought about the mystery plane just then and wondered if we'd see it again that night.

Brandon and Sherlock opened the storage compartment and passed out the fishing gear. "Better check your hook, Penny," Brandon suggested as he gave me a fishing rod and a grin. I growled at him.

I chose the fattest worm in the entire bucket. Biting my lip in disgust, I put him on my hook. "Go for the biggest bass in the whole lake," I whispered to the worm and then sent him sailing across the water. Before he even had time to get his tail wet I felt a hard jerk on my line. I jerked back gently. *Don't let go!* I silently instructed whatever was on the other end. *Hang on tight!* The line suddenly cut through the water in the direction of the bow, and I knew that the fish was following my instructions.

"Penny has one!" Lisa exclaimed.

My heart was pounding furiously as Mr. Diamond leaned over the side with the landing net just moments later. "Bring him in closer, Penny," he coaxed, "just a little closer . . . Got him!" A feeling of relief flooded over me as the millionaire stood up with the struggling fish safely in the net.

"How big is he?" I asked as he lifted my catch from the net to unhook him and put him in the live well.

Mr. Diamond paused. "He's a nice one, Penny. He's at least two pounds." It was the biggest fish I had ever caught, but I was a bit disappointed that he wasn't even larger. I reached in for another worm, and the rest of the crew prepared to make their first cast of the evening.

"The airplane," Sherlock announced. "He's back!"

We all looked up. High overhead, tiny red and white lights were barely visible. The plane was so high that we could not yet hear the plane's engines.

"It's a different plane," Brandon whispered.

"I don't think so," Sherlock replied. "It's the phantom plane." As if to verify Sherlock's words, just then the red and white lights began to blink on and off.

"You were right," Lisa whispered.

From somewhere in the vicinity of Briarwood, a white light blinked in response to the signals from the aircraft high overhead. Sherlock watched intently, and I realized that he was counting the flashes. I glanced up again. The lights on the plane were blinking again.

Suddenly, it hit me. The signals on the ground were coming from Briarwood. Was Senator Greene involved in this operation?

The signals ceased, and we watched in silence as the plane descended with its lights extinguished. We could hear the plane's engines now, which helped us keep track of what was happening.

I saw a silver flash of light as the moonlight reflected off the wing of the plane. Moments later the engines stopped, and we knew that the plane had touched down on the lake. We heard the roar of a boat motor, and a tiny white light went skipping across in the darkness.

"Mr. Diamond, would you take us closer?" Sherlock asked. I felt a whisper of fear run through me, but at the same instant, curiosity raised its head and looked around. *What was Sherlock up to?* I glanced over and, to my surprise, saw that Sherlock had the two million candlepower spotlight in his hand. He must have stashed it in the boat sometime during the afternoon. The cord was plugged into the dashboard of the *Gemstone*. *What in the world?*

"I'd better not, Sherlock," Mr. Diamond said softly. "We don't really know what's going on here. It could be dangerous."

"Two hundred yards," Sherlock begged. "Take us within two hundred yards. They won't hear us over their boat's motor, and the red fiberglass of the *Gemstone*'s hull looks black at night, so they won't see us. Please?"

I held my breath. One part of me was hoping that Mr. Diamond would say "yes" so that Sherlock could do whatever it was that he needed to do, but another part of me was hoping to stay alive awhile longer. "We'll go a little closer," Mr. Diamond finally replied. "But it may be more than two hundred yards." I couldn't decide whether to be relieved or disappointed.

The millionaire started the *Gemstone*'s engine, and we quietly crept closer. My heart was pounding against my rib cage, and I felt a creeping uneasiness at the bottom of my stomach. I was thankful that the moon had ducked behind a cloud, plunging our part of the lake into darkness.

The roar of a boat motor announced the departure of the other boat, and the tiny white light went skipping across toward Briarwood. We still couldn't see the airplane, but we could hear it taxiing toward the end of the lake, away from Briarwood. Mr. Diamond shut the *Gemstone*'s engine down to an idle. "Sorry, Sherlock," he said softly, "I guess we're too late." I thought I detected a note of relief in his voice.

The hum of the airplane's engines increased in pitch and volume as the unseen aircraft sped back across the lake toward Briarwood. Although we could not see the plane, we could tell from the sound when it lifted its pontoons from the water and was airborne. Suddenly Sherlock switched on the powerful spotlight. The beam stabbed through the darkness like a white-hot knife, intense and white and glaring. Sherlock swept the beam across the lake, catching the climbing aircraft in the powerful, blinding light.

"N374FL," he said with a note of satisfaction in his voice. Abruptly, he switched the spotlight off. "That's all we needed."

"What's N . . . 37 . . . whatever?" I asked.

"Aircraft identification numbers," Sherlock replied. "They're displayed on the side of the fuselage. Now I can find out who owns this plane."

Mr. Diamond pushed the throttle lever down, and the *Gemstone* picked up speed. "Sherlock, that was just a bit dangerous," he scolded gently. "I guess I should have asked you what you had in mind before I agreed to go closer."

Neither Mr. Diamond nor I realized it at the time, but Sherlock was already planning an even bolder venture for the following night. And that's when the real danger would come into play.

EIGHT

OUR DISCOVERY

Thursday afternoon I sat alone on the deck, feeding popcorn to a little chipmunk that scampered around my feet. I laughed at the little creature's antics, suddenly feeling cheerful and happy again. I had been just a bit homesick for Mom and Dad. Sure I was having a blast here at Diamond Point with my friends, and I hated to even think of having to leave Thunderbird Lake on Saturday. On the other hand though, I was missing my parents. I had called them twice, but that's still not the same as seeing them.

The little chipmunk gave an indignant little squeaking sound and scurried up on the bench beside me in an effort to get my attention. He had run out of popcorn, and I hadn't noticed. I laughed and reached into the bag. "Sorry," I told him. "Here." I offered a piece of popcorn to him, holding it just a couple of inches above the bench.

The chipmunk studied the popcorn for several seconds. He took two tiny steps toward it and then sat back and looked up at me. It was obvious that he wanted the popcorn but wasn't sure if he could trust me. "Come on," I coaxed in a whisper, "I won't hurt you. Take it."

The chipmunk looked at the popcorn again, then at me, and then at the popcorn again. I held perfectly still.

Slowly, cautiously, the furry little guy crept in and grabbed the popcorn with two tiny paws. But he didn't snatch it and run away, like I expected. Instead, he gently took the popcorn from my outstretched fingers and then sat back and ate it right there, squatting less than an inch from my hand! I held my breath, afraid that I would scare him if I even breathed. I desperately wanted to pick him up and hold him and pet him, but I knew that that was out of the question.

I reached into the bag for another piece. Either the movement of my hand or the noise from the cellophane bag frightened the little creature, for he suddenly leaped down from the bench and dashed away five or six feet. "Sorry," I told him. I tossed several kernels of popcorn on the deck and he came closer, picking up the popcorn and scarfing it down.

My thoughts went back to that morning. We had made another trip back to Aysee's to pick up some light bulbs for Robert. Sherlock had again correctly identified each of the twins—to the puzzlement of us all—but that wasn't what I was thinking about. When Lisa and I had walked down the aisle where they keep the light bulbs, Norm had followed us. I had assumed that he was just coming over to help us, but when he got us alone at the light bulb display, he started asking Lisa some pretty serious questions about the tracts. I was amazed at his sincerity and openness.

When we left the store, Lisa was so excited she was shaking. "He's close, Penny!" she exclaimed delightedly. "He's so close. I've been praying for this for so long." Her eyes filled with tears, and I stared at her in surprise. "Penny, pray for him. He's gonna get saved soon—I know it! Please pray."

I dropped my head as I tossed the chipmunk another kernel of popcorn. When was the last time that *I* shed tears over someone who was unsaved?

Sherlock interrupted my thoughts and scared the chipmunk as he sauntered across the deck toward me. "Guess who the plane is registered to?" he asked me with a grin.

I shrugged. "Who?"

"Superior Waste Management," he replied, with the same tone of voice a lawyer would use to inform a client that he had just inherited millions of dollars.

The information meant nothing to me. "So?"

"Penny, Superior is owned by Northern States Enterprises, which is owned by—guess who?"

A wild idea occurred to me just then, but I went ahead and blurted it out. "Senator Greene!"

"Right! Good thinking, Penny!" Sherlock congratulated me, but I was afraid to tell him that it was just a wild guess.

"How did you find that out?" I asked.

"The ID number on the side of the plane," he explained. "I accessed the FAA database through the Internet to identify the registered owner. Just as I guessed, the plane belongs to Senator Greene."

"I thought you didn't make guesses," I teased.

Sherlock grinned. "This was one of the exceptions. I had a pretty good idea."

He sat down beside me and reached into the popcorn bag. Taking six or seven kernels from the bag, he tossed them to the chipmunk, which had returned to a cautious, respectful distance. The chipmunk crept closer.

"The next step," Sherlock told me, "is to find out what the plane is bringing to Thunderbird Lake each night. I'm sure it's something illegal, or the pilot wouldn't be running in here without lights. The fact that he used the northern side of the lake on the night of the party reinforces that theory. But at this point, I have no clue as to what is being delivered."

"Maybe they're running drugs," I suggested.

"Uh oh, you're guessing, Penny," he chided, and we both laughed.

"I have a plan," he told me. Behind his thick glasses, his eyes burned with an intensity that alarmed me. "I think I've devised a way to get our hands on one of the deliveries."

I took a deep breath. That old familiar feeling of impending danger was returning.

We grilled out again that evening, and the steaks were delicious. Robert served a huge cheesecake—my favorite—for dessert. "I guess there's no fishing trip tonight," Mr. Diamond said as we finished. "I've got a conference call scheduled with one of the divisions of my research and development team."

I glanced at Sherlock and saw a look of utter dismay cross his face. Apparently, the millionaire CEO's announcement had a bearing on the young detective's plans. "Daddy, what about us?" Lisa asked. "Couldn't we go fishing without you?"

Mr. Diamond frowned. "I really don't want you taking the *Gemstone* out at night," he replied.

"We could take the canoes," Lisa reasoned. "We spent a couple of hours in them this morning, and we're getting pretty good with them."

Her father hesitated. "I don't know," he said. "It's Robert's night off, so I really can't ask him to go with you."

"We'll be careful," Lisa pleaded. "We'll stay together, and we'll wear life vests, and . . ."

"OK, OK," Mr. Diamond relented. "As long as you take both canoes, and everyone wears a life vest the entire time. I want you to have a light, and I want you back at ten-thirty."

Heavy clouds were rolling across the moonlit sky, and a slight breeze was kicking up as the two canoes glided silently across the darkness of Thunderbird Lake. Sherlock and I were in the lead canoe, and Brandon and Lisa were following in the other. "What's in your backpack?" I asked, having noticed when Sherlock put it on the floor of the canoe with the fishing rods.

"Just part of my plan," he replied in a voice that told me it was useless to probe further.

It took us twenty minutes of steady paddling to reach the north wing of the lake. We cruised along the west shore around the corner from Briarwood. *The Gemstone would have gotten here in just over a minute,* I realized as we finally stopped to rest. *Give me a wave runner or a powerboat any day!*

I heard a noise in the rear of the canoe and turned around to look. Sherlock was pulling an object out of his backpack, and I was surprised to see that it was the two million candlepower spotlight! "How are you going to power that?" I asked Sherlock. "Canoes don't have batteries."

"No, but motor scooters do," he replied with a grin as he pulled a small battery from the backpack. It looked like a miniature car battery, and I knew that it was twelve volt, just like a car battery. Sherlock pulled some wires and alligator clips from the backpack and hooked the battery to the spotlight. "Mr. Diamond told us to take a light," he said, "and I did."

We paddled for a few more minutes, finally stopping three quarters of a mile north of the senator's mansion. Sherlock looked at his watch. "Twenty-five minutes to get here," he observed. "We have to leave here by 10:05."

Brandon and Lisa floated fifteen feet away as we got out the fishing rods and got serious about fishing. I turned around on my seat so that I was facing Sherlock instead of facing forward.

"I've got dibs on the first fish," Brandon announced.

It was one of those nights. After fishing for an hour and a half, none of us had gotten even a nibble! "Brandon must have cut all the hooks," Lisa joked, "including his own!"

"You can't blame this one on me," Brandon protested good-naturedly. "I think Penny's responsible this time."

The canoes bumped against each other in the darkness. Brandon cleared his throat. "I want to tell you guys something," he said. "I just want you to know that I appreciate . . . that I appreciate you helping me get saved. Especially you, Lisa. If you hadn't given me that little booklet that tells how to receive Jesus, I never would have known about it." His voice grew husky, and he paused. "Thank you," he finished softly.

"We're glad you got saved," Lisa responded.

"Oh, and there's something else I need to tell you," Brandon said nervously. "Sherlock, remember when I knocked you off your bike in the middle of the street a year or two ago? Well, I want you to know that I'm sorry about it."

"That's OK," Sherlock mumbled.

"There's one more thing," Brandon continued. "Would you pray for my mom? She's not saved, and I want . . ." His voice trailed off.

"We will," Lisa promised. "And I want to ask you guys to pray for Norm and Max Aysee too. Norm was talking to me at the store today, and I think he's almost ready to get saved."

We fished in silence for another fifteen minutes. Finally Lisa spoke up. "Let's head back in, shall we? This is just the wrong night to fish."

Sherlock pushed the light button on his watch. "We have twenty more minutes before we absolutely have to head back," he said. "Why don't we wait another fifteen?" I knew that he was still hoping that the phantom airplane would show up.

"Fine with me," Lisa agreed. "How about you guys? Penny? Brandon?" We both agreed, and the matter was settled.

Sherlock grew fidgety during the next few minutes. It seems that he must have pushed the light button on his watch every thirty seconds or so. We were running out of time, but the airplane still hadn't come. Finally he let out a sigh. "Five more minutes," he said with a note of quiet resignation in his voice, "and then we have to head for home."

We all heard the plane's engines at the same instant. I looked up. Sure enough, high overhead, red and white marker lights were visible through the breaks in the clouds. To my surprise, Sherlock pointed his spotlight skyward and began flashing it at the aircraft overhead. "What are you doing?" I hissed at him. "Do you want him to know that we're here?"

"Quiet, please," Sherlock replied, staring intently at the sky. "I have to concentrate."

The plane was blinking its lights. Sherlock watched closely. He gave a series of answering blinks, watched the response from the plane, and then blinked several more times. The plane turned off its lights completely and began to circle in the darkness.

Sherlock put the spotlight away. "Well," he said casually, "if he believed me, we'll soon get an airmail package."

"What?" I couldn't believe my ears. "What did you do?"

"I've watched their signals these last three nights, and I've figured out their code," the young detective explained. "The first sequence of flashes is a security code. It changes every night, but I think I've figured out the pattern. The second sequence told the pilot that we have nothing for him to pick up; he can drop his delivery by parachute instead of risking a landing in the darkness. The last signal told him to drop it here on the north wing instead of on the south wing in front of Briarwood."

I was amazed. "You figured all that out just by watching their flashes?"

I think he shrugged, but it was hard to see in the darkness. "I had three nights," he said, as if that explained his incredible feat.

Two minutes later, the plane overhead flashed its lights twice. A single white light arced through the air high overhead and then began to fall in a straight line. It slowed down abruptly, and I realized that a parachute had opened. "Bingo!" Sherlock said with satisfaction.

He picked up his paddle. "Let's go!" he whispered. "We have to chase our package down!"

I turned around on my seat and picked up my paddle. Side by side, the two canoes glided noiselessly toward the descending light. It disappeared, and we knew that it had reached the water. "Faster!" Sherlock urged.

Three minutes later we approached a blinking light that bobbed in the water. As we pulled alongside, I could make out the white shape that I knew would be the parachute. I reached over the gunwale and grabbed it. Contact!

We found a sturdy cargo net fastened to the parachute, and a waterproof light tied securely to that. Inside the net were several flotation devices to make sure that the cargo would not sink. But what really had our attention—and curiosity—were two large storage totes. They were made of a sturdy, dark green plastic, and their lids were fastened securely closed with duct tape.

Sherlock was busily snipping away at the cargo net with a pair of scissors. *Now how did he know to bring scissors?* I asked myself.

"Grab this tote when it's free," he urged Brandon, who had brought the other canoe along on the opposite side of the whole apparatus. "Help Penny get it in our canoe. I'll have you guys take the second one."

Three minutes later, we had both the totes in the canoes and were paddling back toward shore. We beached the canoes, anxious to see what the totes contained. Sherlock pulled out a tiny pocket flashlight, and we worked feverishly to peel away the duct tape from the first tote. Finally with trembling hands, we opened the lid, and Sherlock flashed the light inside.

"Garbage!" Brandon blurted. "We went through all this for a load of garbage!" It *did* look like it. The tote contained a large, black plastic garbage bag, which was tied securely closed.

"I don't think so," Sherlock said quietly. "Hold my light, Penny." He slashed at the cord securing the sack closed, and with a triumphant flourish, threw the garbage bag wide open. We gasped as we saw the contents. We were staring at bundles of money— stacks and stacks of hundred-dollar bills!

The four of us stood speechless for about thirty seconds as the enormity of what we had just done began to sink in. "Oh, no," Lisa groaned finally. "We're in trouble now! People get killed for a lot less than this."

Sherlock knelt and began to dig through the bundles. "It's hundreds about half of the way down, and then it changes to fifties," he announced. He studied one of the bundles. "This is a bundle of a hundred bills, which would come to ten thousand dollars per bundle." He did some quick figuring in his head. "If

I'm figuring right, this one tote contains almost two million dollars!"

I felt like fainting.

"Let's see what's in the other tote," he said, "and then see about getting this home and calling the police."

"How about leaving this here and just getting out of here alive?" I quavered. "Sherlock, do you realize how much danger we could be in?" I glanced around fearfully. The wind howled like a creature in distress, and suddenly just the idea of being alone in the darkness with several million dollars of someone else's money was absolutely terrifying. "Let's get out of here!"

I don't think he even heard me. He was already down on his knees, ripping the duct tape from the second tote. Seconds later, he eagerly tore off the lid. I shined the tiny light inside. Like the first tote, this one also contained a plastic garbage bag. But there was also a small notebook on top of the garbage bag.

Sherlock snatched it up and flipped it open. "More light, Penny," he said hoarsely.

I focused the light on the notebook and peered over his shoulder, which was easy to do since he's so short. Apparently the little book was some kind of record of financial transactions. The page I saw was filled with dates, numbers, and somebody's initials. The numbers were kind of funny, and they really didn't make any sense. A typical column read something like this: 120k, 480k, 190k, 1.2m, 750k. It didn't make sense. "What does 'k' stand for?" I asked Sherlock. "And what's 'm'?"

"Thousands and millions," he answered absently. His mind was working on something else as he paged slowly through the rest of the little book.

Thousands and millions, I thought. *Thousands and millions of what?* Suddenly, I gasped. The book was referring to dollar amounts, and we weren't talking about pocket change. I trembled with the realization of what we were dealing with.

Brandon had opened the second garbage bag. "It's all twenties," he announced in a hoarse, fearful whisper, "but it's fuller than the other tote."

Sherlock abruptly flipped the little book closed and tossed it into the tote. He knelt and snapped the plastic lid closed. "Let's get these back to Diamond Point," he said. "We'll put one in each canoe."

Lisa shrank from the idea. "I don't want to be in the same canoe with so much money," she whimpered. "What if something happens?"

To my surprise, Brandon agreed with her. "I'd rather not either," he told Sherlock.

"OK, Penny and I will take both totes in our canoe," he said. I guess it never occurred to him that I might feel the same as Lisa and Brandon. At least, he never asked me.

We dragged the totes back to the canoes and deposited them both in our canoe. Hearts pounding, we shoved off and paddled through the darkness toward the south wing of the Thunderbird. I glanced behind us, but could see no sign of Lisa's canoe.

Sherlock and I were just entering the body of the Thunderbird when I heard a sound that sent a bolt of terror through my entire being. A boat motor had just rumbled to life, and the sound was coming from the direction of Briarwood!

We paddled desperately. Fear seemed to cramp my muscles, making it difficult to paddle. My arms felt like lead. *Help us, Lord!* I prayed silently.

Like an angry wasp, the powerful boat came charging across the lake. A finger of brilliant light swept across the surface of the water. The powerful beam crossed over our heads and then swept back in our direction. "Duck!" Sherlock called to me.

It was too late. The searchlight flashed across our bow, hesitated, and then swung back to lock in on our canoe. The powerful white beam blinded me. I heard an angry voice snarl, "Over there!"

The boat came racing in our direction, and the glaring light never left us for an instant. I looked up to see the silhouette of the speedboat bearing down on us, and I actually thought it was going to run us down. The driver veered away at the last possible instant, cutting the engine as he did. Rocking wildly in its own wake, the powerful boat came to a stop just twenty feet from us. Our canoe bobbed up and down, and I thought we were going to capsize.

"You there!" a harsh, angry voice snarled. "Paddle over here!"

I was so paralyzed by fear that I couldn't even move. But the canoe crept toward the speedboat, and through the fog of my terror, I realized that Sherlock was paddling. He slowed as we approached the other boat, and our gunwale bumped the ski platform at the stern with a gentle thump.

We looked up to see two automatic weapons trained on us. The glare of the light kept me from seeing the men very clearly, but I did see the guns. And they were very real.

"They have the totes," a second voice growled, "and the duct tape is gone! They've opened them!" He turned back to his companion. "You know what we have to do."

NINE

CAPTURED!

Sherlock and I were in serious, desperate trouble. We were involved in a nightmare beyond anything I had ever encountered. As I stared up at the blinding glare of the light from the powerboat, my heart seemed to go into shock. Fear paralyzed my diaphragm, and for a few moments, I couldn't even breathe.

"Grab the platform," the man closest to me growled. I stared at his silhouette, my mind senseless with terror, not even comprehending his words. He repeated the command. "Girl, I said to grab the platform! Move!"

Stiff hands that didn't even seem to belong to me reached out and grabbed the redwood ski platform at the stern of the boat.

"You, kid," the man said, gesturing with the gun toward Sherlock, "you grab it too! Hold the canoe steady!" Sherlock knelt in front of his seat and meekly obeyed, pulling the side of the canoe firmly against the edge of the platform.

The other man stepped over the transom of the boat, placing one foot on the ski platform. He leaned down, grabbed one of the plastic totes, and hefted it into the powerboat. The man was tall and bald-headed, but that's all I can tell you about him. He leaned down a second time, lifted the second tote into the boat, and then turned to his companion. "What do we do with the kids?"

The first man shrugged. "They've seen too much." Every nerve in my tense body seemed to leap and shudder at these words. I began to shake uncontrollably.

"Turn them over to Greene and let him decide," the tall man argued. "Let him take the rap for it—not us."

"Better to take care of it now," his companion replied. "And then we sink the canoe."

Just then I realized that tears were streaming down my cheeks.

The tall man looked us over. "Stay here and hang on," he told us. "There's no way you can get away from us, so don't even try. We'll be right here the whole time." Motioning for the other man to follow, he stepped to the bow of the boat, away from us. The two men stood talking in low tones so that we couldn't hear, but Sherlock and I both knew that they were discussing the best way to do away with us.

Lord, help us, I prayed desperately. *Please send somebody to help us!* It didn't take a rocket scientist to figure out that our situation was hopeless. Sherlock and I couldn't fight these guys, and there was no way to try to escape; they would simply follow us. *Lisa and Brandon! They might have seen the powerboat, and they could go for help.* But that hopeful idea evaporated as I realized that it would take them at least fifteen minutes to reach Diamond Point. Sherlock and I simply didn't have that much time.

"Penny. Let go of the platform," Sherlock's urgent whisper cut through the fog of my troubled thoughts. "Let go of the platform."

I shook my head slightly, trying not to move enough so that the men in the boat would notice. *It's no use, Sherlock,* I thought sadly, we *can't simply paddle away and escape. They'll just hunt us down.* But somehow I hadn't remembered just how creative and resourceful a genius can be, even in a time of extreme danger. Sherlock had a plan.

"Penny, let go," he whispered again, softly, urgently. "Let go so I can pull the canoe forward." I released my grip, and the bow of the canoe crept past the left corner of the powerboat.

I glanced at the men. They were deep in an animated discussion and neither seemed to be looking right at us, so I decided it was safe to take a peek at Sherlock. To my surprise, he was down on his knees in the bottom of the canoe, leaning over the gunwale, reaching into the water beneath the ski platform of the powerboat! *What in the world?* Moments later, he straightened to an upright posture and pulled the canoe back where it had been previously. I was mystified by his actions.

At that moment our captors came striding back to the stern of the boat. "We're sorry, kids," the shorter man growled, "but we have to—hey! What in the world? Carl, the stern's filled with water!" He cursed violently. "We're sinking!"

"It's the kids," Carl snarled. "They pulled the drain plugs! We'll have to make a run for the boathouse."

"We can't just leave the kids here."

"Peretti will have our heads if we lose the cash or the boat." Carl shouted as he started the engine. "I'm not taking that chance."

Sherlock gave a mighty push and shoved us free of the stern as the powerful speedboat leaped forward with a roar. The wake from the prop set the canoe to rocking perilously, nearing overturning us. The *Diplomat*—I saw the name across the stern—charged across the lake toward Briarwood.

With tears streaming down my face, I sank to my knees in front of the canoe seat. I was shaking like an aphid about to be devoured by a praying mantis. Laying my head against the gunwale, I sobbed out my thanks to God.

"We have to get out of here, Penny. They'll be coming back." I nodded weakly, too dazed by what had just happened to even remember where my paddle was. The canoe began to glide through the water, but we were heading toward the shore across from Briarwood, instead of toward Diamond Point. "We don't have time to paddle across the lake," Sherlock explained. "We'll ditch the canoe in the woods and walk around the lake."

A white-hot bolt of lightning struck the surface of the lake just then, causing me to jump and scream. The crash of thunder that followed was so loud and so close that you could actually feel it. The wind howled out of the west, sounding like a Tyrannosaurus rex in terrible pain. "Sherlock!" I screamed, "a storm is coming!"

"We're not far from shore," he shouted. "The wind has been blowing us toward the eastern shore for the last ten minutes." Now how would anybody notice that in a time of terror like we had just been through? Sherlock had.

The next flash of lightning showed that Sherlock was right. We were less than fifty yards from shore. Moments later, the canoe grated on the sand, and I gratefully scrambled out. The clouds ripped open, and the rain fell in torrents. We dragged the canoe across the beach and into the trees.

"Where are Lisa and Brandon?" I screamed. "They can't cross the lake in this storm!"

"We have to find them," Sherlock shouted above the noise of the wind. "They're in danger when the men come back."

We ran along the edge of the lake. The next bolt of lightning, a prolonged flash that lasted several seconds and lit up the entire south wing of the lake, showed the silhouette of two figures huddled in a canoe. They were two or three hundred yards farther south, but they were only forty or fifty yards out from shore. Like us, they had been driven toward the eastern shore by the wind.

Sherlock and I sprinted through the darkness. The next flash of lightning showed that we had almost caught up with them. "Lisa!" I screamed above the howl of the wind, "Brandon! Paddle to the shore!"

"Where are you?" came Brandon's voice across the water.

I saw a tiny flash of light beside me and realized that Sherlock was signaling with his pocket flashlight. He never misses a single trick. "Over here!" I called. "Lisa! Over here!" Moments later, the canoe landed on the sand in front of us. Two wet passengers scrambled out, and we helped them drag the craft deep into the woods.

The storm put on a violent, dazzling display of electrical power as we ran through the pelting rain. Fiery bolts of white lightning cut across the blackness of the sky while booming reports of thunder echoed across the lake again and again. The wind shrieked and moaned, driving the rain in gusting sheets across the lake with stinging ferocity. I had never seen a storm like it. It was almost terrifying, and yet, in a way, it was awesome!

Fifteen minutes later, we reached Diamond Point. Robert and Mr. Diamond met us at the door wearing raincoats and carrying huge flashlights. "Where have you been?" Mr. Diamond demanded, giving Lisa a stern look. "You're twenty minutes late, and we were worried sick. We were just heading out to look for you."

"Sir, it's my fault that they're late," Sherlock spoke up. "We had to ditch the canoes and walk around the lake. It wasn't safe to cross tonight."

A dazzling bolt of lightning streaked across the sky just then, and the resulting clap of thunder shook the huge glass windows in the entryway. Mr. Diamond glanced in the direction of the lake and then back at us as we stood shivering and dripping on the polished marble floor. "No, I guess not," he replied, and his expression softened. "Better get out of those wet clothes. Robert and I will whip up some hot chocolate to warm you up."

Five minutes later, Lisa and I slipped into the upstairs den. Sherlock and Brandon were already there, sipping hot chocolate and talking to the two men. Mr. Diamond looked up as we entered. "Lisa, light the fire, would you? I forgot."

I glanced at the cold, dead fireplace. *A nice roaring fire would be great right now,* I thought. *Too bad Mr. Diamond didn't already have it going.* To my surprise, Lisa walked to the fireplace and flipped a switch on the wall. Instantly, the fireplace was filled with a cheerful, crackling blaze. I stared in fascinated amazement. *Automatic fireplaces? What is this high-tech world coming to?*

"Sir, we were in over our heads," Sherlock was saying. In the next two minutes, he recounted the events of the evening, beginning with the return of the phantom airplane and concluding with the sudden storm on the lake. He even told of the men who had taken the money away from us, but he didn't mention that they both had guns. The millionaire and the caretaker sat silently listening through the entire account, their eyes wide with astonishment. Maimee slipped into the room just as Sherlock finished and silently took a seat beside Robert.

"Three million dollars, huh?" Mr. Diamond boomed, shaking his head in disbelief.

Sherlock nodded. "That's just a quick estimate."

"You kids have gotten yourselves involved in something big. Mighty big!" He turned to Robert. "Get me the phone."

"Sir, wait, please," Sherlock begged, unwittingly grabbing Mr. Diamond's arm. "Don't call the police yet. I need another day to figure the rest of this out. I don't quite have all the clues that I need."

"We have to call them, son," Robert rasped. "It sounds as if a crime is being committed."

"And three million dollars is involved," Mr. Diamond added.

"Yes, but these are daily deliveries," Sherlock reasoned. "There'll be another one tomorrow. All I need is one more day. We can call the police tomorrow night."

"Do you know where the money came from?" the millionaire asked.

"It's a money laundering operation," the boy detective replied. "Unless I'm mistaken, the money is coming from crime syndicates on both the east and west coasts."

"What's money laundering?" I asked. I had a mental picture of gangsters loading a bushel of hundred-dollar bills into a washing machine and putting it on the permanent press cycle. "Hold the bleach, Tony!"

"Money involved in a crime can often be traced by the serial numbers," Mr. Diamond explained, "whether it's drug money, illegal gambling receipts, cash from a robbery, whatever. When the money is traced back to the criminal, it can be used as evidence to obtain a conviction. A person who 'launders' money simply replaces it with bills that are 'clean,' or not traceable to any illegal activity. The 'dirty' money is either withdrawn from circulation for awhile, or introduced in an area where it won't be suspect, perhaps one of the foreign markets."

"But the person who takes the dirty money is running a big risk," I declared. "Why would they want to do that?"

"They charge a sizeable percentage," Mr. Diamond explained, "sometimes as high as twenty-five percent."

Suddenly the whole thing made sense. I now understood why someone would be willing to take the risks with the "dirty" money. Twenty-five percent of three million is seven hundred and fifty thousand! I looked at Sherlock. "How do you know that this is a money laundering operation? Maybe it was a huge drug deal."

Sherlock shook his head. "We had one of their record books, Penny. The names were in code, but you saw the entries and the amounts. It's definitely money laundering."

He looked at Mr. Diamond with a pleading expression on his thin face. "Please wait until tomorrow afternoon to call the police. I need just one day. I have to try to find out if Senator Greene is involved or if his staff is running the operation without his knowledge."

Mr. Diamond thought it over for several minutes. Finally he shook his head and then strode over to the credenza and picked up the phone. After holding it to his ear for a few seconds, he turned to us with an amused expression on his face. "Phone's not working," he said, hanging up the instrument. "The storm must have knocked it out. I guess we wait till tomorrow after all." He gave us a stern look. "But one thing for sure—nobody goes out again on the lake after dark without me! Is that understood?"

Sherlock was alone in the burgundy dining room the next morning when I came down for breakfast. One glance at his face and I knew that he was in a dark mood. I sat down beside him.

"What's wrong? You look like a funeral director planning his own funeral."

He looked at me as if he had just realized that I was even in the room. When he's concentrating on a problem, he can make himself oblivious to everything else around him. I knew what he was thinking about. "What's wrong?" I asked again.

"I need some way to tie the senator in to this money laundering thing," he mumbled. "If it's like everything else he does, he's insulated himself from it. If his staff is arrested, they take the rap, but he goes free."

"What if he's not involved?" I suggested. "Maybe his staff is running the operation from Briarwood, but he's not even aware of it."

Sherlock shrugged. "That's a possibility," he agreed, "but I don't think so. I've got a hunch that he's the head honcho." He took a green pen from his pocket and began to toy with it. "Over half of the entries in the notebook last night were recorded by a person with the initials 'AR.' If I could get a sample of Senator Greene's handwriting, I could compare it with the writing in the log book."

"Why would it say 'AR' if it's the senator?" I asked. "Wouldn't it be 'AG,' for Adam Greene?"

"His middle name is Richard," Sherlock replied, "so that would fit. Adam Richard." He frowned. "I have to come up with a way to get him to write down some numerals so I can compare them with the numerals in the book. I can see the writing right now as clearly as if I had the book in my hand, but I wish we could have kept the book as evidence."

Lisa stepped into the dining room just then. "Good morning, you two! Hey, did you know it's Daddy's birthday? Robert's making him a cheesecake, and we're going to sing to him at lunch."

Sherlock nudged me, and I saw that funny look in his eyes that means he's up to something. "Mr. Diamond is going to get a birthday card," he whispered mysteriously, "from the senator."

We spent a couple of hours that morning at Mrs. Pendergrass's farm, helping her with her fall canning. Lisa and I peeled apples and vegetables until I thought our fingers would fall off. Even the boys helped, bringing boxes of empty jars down from the attic and washing them in preparation for the canning process. It was a lot of work, but it also was a lot of fun. Mrs. Pendergrass is such a fun person to be around; she's cheerful and happy no matter what she's doing.

"Birthday cards?" Max Aysee said, scratching his head. "Yeah, we got 'em."

Lisa grinned at Sherlock. "Told ya!"

Two minutes later Mr. Aysee stood at the cash register to ring up Sherlock's selection. "Tell you what, Sherlock. I'll discount the card fifty percent if you'll tell me how you knew I was Max."

Sherlock grinned. "I guess I'll pay full price then, won't I?"

"You're gonna do what?" I demanded of Sherlock. "I can't believe you! You're just gonna walk up to Senator Greene and say, 'Excuse me senator, but I need a sample of your handwriting so that I can determine whether or not you're guilty of a crime?' Sherlock, you may have more than your fair share of intelligence, but sometimes I think you could use a little common sense. Are you forgetting last night? No, I won't go to Briarwood with you!"

"Mr. Diamond's birthday is the perfect opportunity," Sherlock insisted. "Nothing can happen to us. Penny, we're going in broad daylight."

"I'm not going, and that's final!" I declared flatly. "And I don't think you should go either."

Twenty minutes later, I was bouncing along on a wave runner speeding toward Briarwood. Sherlock was twenty feet away on the other one. When will I ever learn?

The day was bright and sunny, without a trace of a cloud in the sky. The air was just a bit cooler than it had been yesterday, but the lake was calm. It was almost hard to believe that a storm had raged in tempestuous fury just hours ago in this very spot. Other than a few trees that had fallen along the shoreline as evidence of the violence of the wind, the storm could have simply been a figment of my imagination. The water of the lake was as clear as ever.

I sighed as I thought about the fact that this was our last full day at Thunderbird Lake. Tomorrow afternoon we'd be going home to Willoughby. I glanced behind me and saw two canoes making their way across the lake toward Diamond Point. Sherlock and I had dropped Lisa and Brandon off to pick up the canoes.

I pulled the wave runner closer to Sherlock's. "What if the senator's not home?" I shouted.

"He is!" Sherlock yelled back. "Look!"

I glanced toward Briarwood just in time to see a red and white airplane diving straight toward us! Leaning hard into an evasive right turn, I looked over my shoulder and saw the plane pull up just enough to keep from hitting Sherlock. But the aircraft had a wingspan of only six or seven feet. I realized that it was a radio-controlled model. The plane did a series of loops and barrel rolls just above the water and then headed back toward Briarwood.

As we approached Briarwood, we saw Senator Greene. He was standing on the deck above the boathouse, holding a black-and-silver radio transmitter. The senator was flying the plane!

Sherlock and I tied up at the dock and then hurried up the steep steps to the deck. A man with a build like Mr. Universe hurried toward us. "Get lost, kids. You're on private property!"

Sherlock simply stepped around the man and approached the senator, pulling his birthday card from a plastic bag as he did. "Good morning, Senator," he said politely. "Would you have time to do us a favor? Today is Larry Diamond's birthday, and I was wondering if you would mind signing his card."

Senator Greene did not even glance at us. His attention was on the little airplane. Still watching the sky, he cursed and then growled, "Nick, get rid of these kids." The body-builder stalked toward us.

"Senator, Larry Diamond is CEO of Diamond Computer." Sherlock was talking fast. "Your signature on his birthday card just might be good PR for you!"

I saw an immediate change in the senator's attitude. He held up one hand in Nick's direction as if to stop him and then handed the radio transmitter to him. "Keep it flying." He turned to us, suddenly all smiles and warmth and friendliness. If I had not seen him just seconds before, I would have thought that he was the kindest, gentlest man who ever lived. The change was that abrupt. "I'm sorry," he purred, "I'm afraid that I was a bit preoccupied for a moment." He smiled again. "Once I get my hands on that radio control, it seems that nothing else matters. I'm sorry. Now, what can I do for you?"

Sherlock held out the card. "We were hoping that you would sign Mr. Diamond's birthday card."

"Of course. Glad to." Smiling beneficently, Senator Greene pulled out a pen and signed. I got a cold, creepy feeling deep inside as I watched him.

Sherlock glanced at the card and then held it out again. "Would you mind dating it for him? Uh, let's see, this is ten-seventeen, two thousand and..."

Greene laughed as he cut him off. "I know the date, son." I noticed that the legislator wrote in numerals just as Sherlock had said. He handed the card back to Sherlock. "Is there anything else?"

"No sir, and thank you, sir," Sherlock replied politely. "We appreciate your time."

"Glad to do it, son, glad to do it. Have a great day, and wish my friend Mr. Diamond a happy birthday for me." He gave us both a warm, grandfatherly smile as he took the airplane controls back from Nick. The red and white airplane did loops and spins over our heads as we sped back to Diamond Point.

We parked the wave runners in the Diamond's boathouse before Sherlock even looked at the card. He opened the envelope eagerly and held the card less than twelve inches from his thick glasses. I waited impatiently but in silence. Finally he lowered the card.

"That was the senator's handwriting, all right," he said quietly. "The numerals in today's date match many of the numerals in the log book. The seven, for instance. The senator writes it in a very unusual fashion, but that's exactly the way many of the sevens were written in the book! And the 'A' in Adam matches the initial in the book perfectly."

He sighed and looked at me with a hurt, disappointed expression on his thin face. "Senator Greene *is* involved, Penny. Now we have to find a way to prove it."

TEN

THE MOTOR HOME

Sherlock presented the birthday card to Mr. Diamond right after lunch in the upper-level dining room, just as Robert was serving a huge cheesecake festooned with candles. Lisa gave her father a small gift wrapped in sapphire blue foil paper, which turned out to be an electronic Bible. "It's King James Version," Mr. Diamond observed as he opened the package. "Good."

We all sang "Happy Birthday" to him and then dug into the cheesecake.

Mr. Diamond opened Sherlock's card. "Signed by Senator Greene," he noted. "Pretty impressive! How did you get this?"

Sherlock just grinned.

As I was eating my wedge of cheesecake, I noticed my little chipmunk friend sitting on the far corner of the deck by the telescope, so I slipped out and went over to him. To my disappointment, the chipmunk leaped across to a tree, scampered down the trunk, and disappeared under the deck. *Oh, well,* I thought,

*I'll just eat this cheesecake by myself! And I was going to share
with you.*

I stood up and placed my dessert plate on the deck railing
and peered through the telescope as I savored the next bite of
Robert's delicious cheesecake. I focused the instrument on Briarwood. A cold chill went over me. The beautiful property now
seemed like the castle of an evil king, a symbol of tyranny and
destruction.

The telescope seemed almost to drop by itself, and I found
myself looking at the boathouse. Two men came out just then,
and I let out a tiny gasp of surprise. They were carrying the
two green plastic totes from last night! While I watched, they
crossed behind the boathouse and carried the totes over to the
motor home parked at the edge of the woods. I trembled with
excitement.

Looking up from the telescope, I saw that Sherlock was
watching me through the huge window, so I motioned for him to
come out. "You won't believe what just happened," I whispered
to him. "Two men carried the money totes from the boathouse to
the motor home. They're in there now!"

Sherlock peered eagerly through the instrument. "Were they
the ones from last night?"

"I'm sure of it," I whispered. "They were made of dark green
plastic—"

"The men, Penny, the men. Were they the ones from last
night?"

"Oh," I mumbled, feeling foolish. "I'm not sure. All I noticed was that they had the totes and that they took them to the
motor home."

I waited in silence for several minutes as Sherlock watched
through the telescope. Suddenly he tensed slightly, and I knew
that something was up. "What's happening?" I whispered.

"They just came out of the motor home," he whispered. "They don't have the totes with them." He moved to one side. "Take a look. Are those the men that had the totes?"

I studied the backs of the men as they walked toward the mansion. "That's them."

"Are you sure?"

"Well, not really," I admitted, "but I think so."

Sherlock studied Briarwood for several moments through the telescope. "Watch the motor home," he told me as he stepped away from the instrument. "I need to know if anyone goes in or comes out. I'll be right back." I took his place peering through the telescope.

He was back in forty seconds with his walkie-talkies and Brandon. "Penny and I need you to watch Briarwood," he told Brandon, switching one of the walkie-talkies on and handing it to him. "Radio us immediately if anyone heads for the motor home."

Brandon took the walkie-talkie and leaned down to peer through the telescope. "Gotcha!"

Sherlock turned the other unit on. "Come on, Penny."

I followed him as he dashed toward the boathouse. "Where are we going?"

"We're going to see if we can find the record book from the money laundering," he answered, pressing the button that lowered one of the wave runners into the water. "I'm almost positive that it's in the motor home."

I drew back. "You're going to go into the motor home?"

He nodded.

"No way! Sherlock, you're crazy! We almost got killed last night, and now you want to go back and ask for more!"

The electric winch had lowered the wave runner into the water, so Sherlock unsnapped the slings. He climbed aboard and started the motor. "Come on, Penny."

"Sherlock, wait. Think this through. We could—"

"Penny, there isn't time to argue! Come on."

I guess you know what happened even before I tell you. Yes, I got on the back of the wave runner although to this day I can't tell you why. Sherlock gunned the engine and we went speeding across the lake toward Briarwood. I noticed that he stayed close to the south shore instead of cutting directly west across the lake. When we came to the Little Bear River, he turned into it to my surprise. He pulled up to the bank and tied the wave runner to a tree overhanging the water.

We both scrambled off. My heart was pounding. Sherlock pulled the walkie-talkie from his belt. "Brandon, do you read me? Over."

"Brandon here. I read you loud and clear. Over."

"Has anyone gone near the motor home? Over."

"Not a soul, Sherlock. Over."

"Thanks, Brandon. Stand by. Over and out." Sherlock clipped the unit to his belt again and pulled his windbreaker down over it.

I followed my skinny friend up the hill through the dense underbrush. "We'll come out of the woods just below the motor home," he said over his shoulder. "We only have to cross about forty feet of open lawn."

Four or five minutes later we paused at the edge of the woods. The motor home was less than twenty yards away. "Brandon, you still there? Over."

"Everything's all clear," Brandon's voice replied. "Over."

"Stand by; we're going in. Over and out."

We're going in. It sounded like we were a team of Navy Seals about to embark on a dangerous mission. There were only two problems: we weren't Navy Seals, and we had no way to defend ourselves. I reached for Sherlock to tell him that we shouldn't do it, but he had already stepped out of the trees and was slipping across the lawn, expecting me to follow. There was nothing else for me to do except try to catch up.

We reached the motor home without incident. Sherlock reached up and grabbed the door latch, and to my surprise the door was unlocked. As we hurried inside the vehicle, all of my inner warning systems went off at once. *You shouldn't be doing this, Penny,* I told myself. *Get out now, while you still can.* But I ignored my fears and closed the motor home door behind me, feeling that I was closing off our only avenue of escape.

The interior of the motor home was gorgeous! We were in the living room, standing on carpet that swallowed you up to your knees. There were lots and lots of etched glass mirrors, fancy chandeliers, and a humongous big-screen TV. The uphol-stery on the furniture was thicker than it needed to be. I stepped back toward the kitchen. *Mom would love to see this,* I thought, as I surveyed the luxurious cherry cabinets, the gleaming brass fixtures, and the beautiful hardwood floor. *Must be nice to be a legislator, and let the taxpayers buy your vehicles.*

"Here they are!" Sherlock exclaimed, and the sound of his voice snapped me back to reality. The place was impressively beautiful, but we were here to do a job and get out. The less time we spent in the senator's motor home, the better. Sherlock was down on his knees, pulling a green tote from under the dining table. He tore the lid off like a kid opening his first present at Christmas. But the tote was empty.

Sherlock dived for the other tote. But it was empty, also. "Look for the notebook, Penny." Sherlock urged me. "Check the cabinets."

I opened the polished cherry cabinet over the marble sink. It was empty—except for the notebook we were after! I couldn't believe it! "Sherlock, look!" I snatched it up.

Sherlock grabbed it from my hand. "Fantastic, Penny! Now, let's get out of here." He stooped and shoved the plastic totes back under the table.

At that moment the walkie-talkie on his belt crackled to life. "Sherlock!" Brandon's voice was frantic. "They're coming! Get out of there!"

Sherlock and I ran for the front door. But Brandon's voice cut in again, urgent, compelling. "Sherlock! They'll see you if you open the door! Find some place to hide!"

Hearts frantic with terror, we turned and dashed for the back of the motor home. We passed the bathroom—the door was open—and found ourselves in a bedroom. There was a queen-sized bed in the center of the room. Sherlock leaped to the foot of the bed and lifted, and the whole thing came up on those little lift rods like you see on the tailgate of a minivan. Looking in, I saw the top of a huge diesel engine. Sherlock slammed the bed back down. "No hiding place here."

We heard the front door open, and I felt as if my heart had stopped. Sherlock slid a full-length mirror to one side, and we saw a good-sized closet, which was empty except for one cardboard box. Perfect! We scrambled inside and slid the door closed as quietly as possible. Sherlock turned his walkie-talkie off.

Peering through the crack in the door, we discovered that we could see the front of the motor home reflected in the mirror over the headboard. The two men were sitting at the dining table, and I could see the totes sitting on the floor in the hallway. I froze as Sherlock slid the closet door open an inch or so.

"I tell you, I'm getting tired of the whole operation," one of the men said, and Sherlock and I looked as each other as we recognized the voice. It belonged to Carl, the tall man from the boat last night! "I'm thinking of checking out."

"You're making good money," the other man replied. "So what's the problem?"

"We're the ones running all the risks, Webb, but Greene gets the lion's share of the take."

Webb cursed. "You don't think he's running risks? He has more at stake than we do. If this thing ever blew up in our faces, he'd lose his senate seat!"

Carl snorted. "Hardly. The press would cover for him, but we'd just get hung out to dry. And he's not running the risks that you think he is. He keeps his bases covered. Take this motor home, for instance. It's registered in my name, so who catches the heat if we have a bust and they find the stuff? I do! And then the senator would claim that I was merely a guest and that he was unaware of my involvement. He's slick, that one."

"That's Carl Underwood," Sherlock whispered right in my ear. "The motor home is registered to him."

"How do you know that?" Even when I whispered, my voice trembled.

"I checked through the Department of Motor Vehicles the first day we came to Diamond Point."

The men were silent for a moment or two, and I got the idea that they were working on something together. Paperwork, maybe, because I could hear them shuffling papers.

"You saying that you want out, Carl?" Webb's voice was hard, cold, and dangerous, like the edge of a knife.

"I'm not saying that, but I am thinking about it."

The men worked quietly for the next several minutes. Sherlock and I waited anxiously. There was no way to get out of here until Carl and Webb left, and they seemed in no hurry to do that. Suddenly I heard the grinding of a starter from under the bed and then the deep rumble of the big diesel engine! One of the men had started the motor home!

"We have to get out of here, Sherlock," I whispered frantically. "This thing is going somewhere!"

"Maybe not right away," he replied. "This motor is diesel. They may let it warm up before they take off. But we can't get out of here unless they leave for a minute."

The big diesel engine rumbled away for fifteen or twenty minutes while we waited anxiously in the closet. Vibrations from the throbbing engine made the closet floor tremble and buzz so that it felt like we were sitting on a riding lawn mower with a bad engine mount. I heard the sudden hiss of air brakes, and the heavy vehicle lurched backward.

The motor home swayed from side to side as it left Briarwood behind. The motion threw me against Sherlock and threw him against the closet wall. It was hard to sit still. I got to my knees and braced myself between the closet door and the back wall.

You can imagine what the ride was like as the motor home negotiated the twisting, winding road that leads up from Thunderbird Lake. Every time the vehicle swayed I banged my head against the wall. After twenty minutes of such torture, the road straightened out, and the swaying, rocking motion stopped. We were out of the worst of the hills, and I knew we had reached the county highway.

The closet door opened so abruptly that it caught us both by surprise. We found ourselves staring up into the startled, angry face of Carl Underwood. It's hard to know who was more shocked: Carl or Sherlock and me.

ELEVEN

CAPTIVES

My heart sank as Carl took us to the front of the motor home. Webb glanced over at us as we appeared beside the driver's seat, and his mouth actually fell open. He cursed and then growled, "Where'd they come from?"

"They were hiding in the bedroom closet," Carl snapped. "They're the same kids from last night." Webb shot him a puzzled glance. "Lucas and I were waiting for the plane to set down in front of Briarwood," Carl explained, "and instead we saw a parachute come down on the north wing of the lake. So we took the *Diplomat* over to check it out. What do we find? These two kids are in a canoe, and they have the money totes with them. Lucas and I recovered everything though."

Webb cursed again as he steered the motor home through a gentle curve. "You should have told me!"

"Lucas and I didn't think it mattered," Carl said lamely.

"Of course, it matters!" Webb shouted. "Since when do you make these decisions?"

Carl shrugged.

"Take them back and lock them in the bathroom," Webb snarled. I could tell that he was really angry with Carl.

"Lock them in? How?"

"Put the kids in the bathroom and close the door," Webb said, as if he were explaining matters to a child. "Wedge the two totes side by side in the hallway. They won't be able to open the bathroom door."

It wasn't until Sherlock and I were locked in that I started to cry. I had tried to hold back, but it was just too much. Now I couldn't help myself. "Oh, Sherlock," I wailed, "they're gonna kill us! Mom and Dad will never even know what happened to me!"

Sherlock's face was grim. "I'm sorry, Penny," he whispered hoarsely. "I shouldn't have gotten you into this." He hung his head. "This is all my fault. I thought I could outsmart these guys."

Suddenly, instead of feeling sorry for myself, I found myself feeling sorry for Sherlock. "Isn't there something in my contract," I said, trying to be lighthearted and make him feel better, "that says I only have to risk my life one time on each case with you? This is the second time this week."

"Oh, Penny," he whispered, and to my surprise his eyes filled with tears. He reached out and gently squeezed my hand. "I'm sorry, Penny."

"We can still pray," I whispered, trying to stifle my own tears.

Sherlock and I held the most unusual prayer meeting in all of history. I was sitting on the lid of the little toilet, and Sherlock was sitting on the floor with his feet up against the shower door, but we poured out our hearts to the Lord.

Sherlock turned his walkie-talkie on and tried to reach Brandon, but there was no answer. Either we were out of range or the metal body of the motor home was interfering with the radio signal. At any rate, he didn't get through.

"I've been wondering about something," I told Sherlock. "What about the fisherman who ran from us? Did you ever find out who he is?"

Sherlock cleared his throat. "I shouldn't tell you his name, but he's a witness in an extortion case pending against a man and woman on Senator Greene's staff. He was in a government witness protection program and was living in an isolated cabin just north of the Thunderbird."

"Bad choice of location for a protected witness in a case involving Senator Greene's staff," I observed dryly.

Sherlock nodded. "Exactly. The agents who placed him had no idea that Senator Greene lived here."

"Wait," I blurted. "How do *you* know all this?"

"I got a good telephoto shot of the man," Sherlock replied, "and faxed it to Agent Meadows with the FBI. Remember Meadows?"

"The FBI agent in charge of Lisa's kidnapping case," I replied.

"Right. Anyway, when Meadows found out who the man was, and that he was hiding out so close to Briarwood, the FBI moved him to another location immediately."

The motor home downshifted, and the swaying and bouncing started again. We both knew that the vehicle had turned off the main highway. The thought made my heart beat faster. I looked up at the skylight over our heads and was surprised to see that it was dark outside. Apparently, we had been in the motor home longer than I realized.

"Stand up, Penny." I wasn't sure what Sherlock had in mind, but I got to my feet. He stepped up on top of the toilet lid, and I noticed that he had his Swiss Army knife in his hand. While I watched in silence, he started taking the screws out of the sky-light in the bathroom ceiling!

There were at least a dozen screws in the molding around the skylight, but Sherlock had them out in less than two minutes. When he pulled on the molding, it came free in his hands! He handed it to me, and I set it on the floor. Sherlock climbed up on the vanity counter, placed both hands against the Plexiglas of the skylight, and pushed with all his might. To my delight, the skylight disappeared into the darkness and the noise of rushing air filled the bathroom, sounding like somebody had just rolled down a window in a moving car.

The opening in the ceiling was roughly fourteen by twenty-four inches, and it suddenly occurred to me that it was large enough for us to slip through, if the motor home ever stopped. I looked up to see that Sherlock was pulling himself through it, but the motor home was still moving! "Sherlock, be careful," I called softly. His reply was lost in the noise of the wind.

A worrisome thought suddenly occurred to me. *What if Carl or Webb hear the noise of the wind? They'll know we're up to something.*

Sherlock had completely disappeared through the skylight, and now his head popped down through the opening. "Come on, Penny, here's our way out!" The motor home swayed and bounced just then, and Sherlock clutched at the side of the sky-light aperture.

"Sherlock, you're crazy!" I protested. "I'm not gonna climb on top of a moving motor home! Wait until it stops!"

"That may be too late," he argued softly. "Come on. There's an air conditioning unit about three feet behind this opening, and I have my legs braced against it. Just behind the air conditioner is the luggage rack, which will provide us with excellent hand-holds all the way back to the ladder. It's a bit scary, but we can do it. We have to!"

Climbing through the open skylight was not one of the high points in my life. The motor home was only doing about thirty-five or forty, but it leaned and swayed every time it swept around a curve, and there were plenty of them. I think Webb was driving too fast for that road. Anyway, I stood on the counter like Sherlock had done and, reaching up, pulled myself through the skylight. Sherlock grabbed hold of my jacket and pulled until I was out far enough to get a grip on the air conditioner. Holding desperately to the railing of the luggage rack, we crawled to the very back of the swaying vehicle.

Moments later the motor home slowed, swept into a left turn, and came to a complete stop with a scraping, grinding sound. Webb was attempting to drive the huge vehicle up a steep, narrow gravel lane leading away from the road, and the back of the motor home was dragging on the asphalt. Sherlock scrambled down the ladder. "Come on, Penny! This is our chance!"

Twenty seconds later, we were standing in the middle of the dark, deserted roadway. The motor home continued up the gravel lane without us. "I'd like to see Carl's face when he opens the bathroom door," Sherlock snickered.

We started hiking down the deserted roadway. Sherlock pulled out his miniature flashlight and switched it on. The beam was tiny, but it helped. Sherlock turned his walkie-talkie on and tried to reach Brandon. "Brandon, do you read me? Over."

There was no answer.

He tried again. "Brandon, do you read me? This is Sherlock. Over." With a sigh, he switched the unit back off. "That's what I thought. We're out of range."

We walked for about five minutes and only passed one house. It was dark, so we didn't stop, but Sherlock paused and shined his flashlight on the mailbox at the side of the road. Moments later we heard a noise and looked back. Headlights sped toward us. We hurried to the side of the road, but Sherlock waved his little flashlight back and forth in an effort to stop the car. The car swept past us in the darkness. But then we saw the red glow of brake lights, and the car backed up to us. The passenger window rolled down noiselessly, and we saw an elderly man and woman. They must have been at least forty-five or fifty years old.

"What are you kids doing out here?" the woman asked.

"We need to get to Comanche," Sherlock replied. "Are you going anywhere near there?"

"We're going in that general direction," the man replied. "Hop in. We'll take you part of the way there. But you kids are too young to be hitchhiking."

We rode with them for about forty minutes. Finally, the man pulled to the side of the road. "We turn here, so if I take you any farther, I'll be taking you away from Comanche. I hate to let you out in such a dark place. Please, don't try hitchhiking after this. It's too dangerous!" We thanked them and climbed out, and the car sped away.

Another car came along two minutes later. Once again, Sherlock used the tiny flashlight to signal the vehicle to a stop. We both hurried over to the driver's window. "Need a ride, huh?" the driver called. "Hop in."

Sherlock and I froze in terror at the sound of the man's voice. It was Lucas, Carl Underwood's partner in the *Diplomat!* I turned to run, but a man appeared around the corner of the car with an automatic in his right hand. "You heard the man," he said, grinning as if the whole episode was a big joke. "Hop in. We can't let you walk home in the dark."

We climbed into the back seat, and Lucas climbed in with us. The man with the gun took the driver's seat. Lucas turned to us as the car sped away into the darkness. "Where's the notebook?" he demanded. "Carl told us that you took it from the motor home."

My heart sank. Carl must have gotten on the CB or cell phone as soon as they discovered that we had escaped from the bathroom. But how could they have discovered so quickly that the notebook was missing?

"We don't have it any longer," Sherlock replied. "I tossed it in the ditch miles ago."

Both men cursed. "Search him, Lucas," the driver growled.

Sherlock took off his windbreaker and handed it to Lucas. "We don't have it. See?" He raised both arms and turned from side to side so that the man could see he wasn't hiding anything.

Lucas looked at me. I had my windbreaker off in less than three seconds. Lucas looked at the other man. "They don't have it."

"We'll never find it," the driver said and cursed again. Every time they talked like that, I hurt inside. Why do people have to use the Lord's name that way? Mr. Diamond says that profanity is the sign of a weak mind, and I think he's right.

Ten minutes later the driver pulled to the side of the road. "Let's put them in the trunk," he told Lucas. "We're getting on the freeway soon, and we can't take the chance of them signaling somebody."

Lucas pulled his gun and pointed it at us. "Come on, let's go."

It was a horrible feeling when the trunk lid closed and the little light went out. Sherlock and I were lying on our sides with our backs to each other, but at least our hands weren't tied. The car started forward, and I began to cry again. Sherlock switched on his little flashlight. "Better save the batteries," I advised him, even thought I desperately wanted the light on. "We might need the light later."

"This will just take a minute," he replied. I heard a noise and twisted around so that I could see what he was doing. A second light blinked on, and our prison grew brighter. Sherlock had pulled one of the car's taillights from the black plastic housing and was using it to light the trunk. Moments later, he had the other taillight inside the trunk. He grinned at me. "Maybe they'll get a ticket for driving without taillights."

"Use your walkie-talkie," I suggested. "See if you can raise Brandon. I'm sure you noticed this car's license number."

"Good thinking, Penny," he responded, "but I couldn't, even if we were within range. I ditched the walkie-talkie with the notebook so I wouldn't take a chance on losing it." The statement didn't make sense to me, but I was too distraught to ask for an explanation.

Five minutes later we felt the car accelerate to a higher speed, and suddenly we heard the noise of other vehicles. We were on the freeway.

Sherlock pulled a wire from one of the bulbs and then pushed the bulb back into its socket in the rear end of the car. He touched the wire to the bulb, took it away, and then touched it again. "What are you doing?" I asked.

"Sending an SOS," he whispered. "Morse code. Pray that someone notices and calls the police." I began to pray, and Sherlock began flashing his message. Fifteen minutes later I was giving up hope, but he was still dutifully flashing.

We both heard the siren at the same time. "It worked!" I rejoiced. "It worked!"

I winced as I heard the men inside the car cursing. "Do we run for it?" Lucas asked.

"We'd never make it," the driver replied. "It's probably just a routine traffic check, so don't worry." He raised his voice. "You kids lie still back there, and don't make a sound, or we'll kill you!"

We felt the car slow and pull to the side of the road. Sherlock continued his flashing. I lay quietly, listening intently. We heard the crunch of gravel underfoot as someone walked past the rear of the car. Sherlock went crazy. He started shouting and beating on the underside of the trunk lid with both hands. "Watch out!" he shouted. "They're both armed!"

I heard a man's voice shout, "Both of you out of the car! Hands over your heads! Keep those hands in the air!" Sherlock stopped shouting, but continued knocking. Moments later, the trunk lid opened, and we were staring up into the world's brightest flashlight.

"You kids OK?" the officer asked us. When we sat up he gave us a huge grin. "Next time try riding inside the car," he advised. "It's a lot more comfortable."

I reached out and hugged him and then started crying again.

TWELVE

LAST DAY AT DIAMOND POINT

The next day was Saturday, and Mr. Diamond let us sleep in until almost nine-thirty. In a way I hated to see this day come because it meant that we had to leave the beauty of Thunderbird Lake and return to dreary little Willoughby. At the same time though, I was glad we were going home. Last night had been just a little too much for me.

We had stayed up till nearly midnight. Sherlock and I had to answer about a million questions about the senator's money laundering operation and about our unexpected trips in the motor home and in the car trunk. The police were treating both incidents as kidnappings even though we had entered the motor home "of our own free will." As the lieutenant pointed out, Carl and Webb didn't release us when they found out that we were on board.

The motor home was "clean," with absolutely no evidence of the money laundering that took place inside. Really the only bit of evidence that Sherlock and I even had to back up our story was the notebook that we had taken from the motor home. As it turned out, Sherlock had noted the address on the mailbox before he tossed the notebook and walkie-talkie in the ditch, so the police were able to find the notebook easily. And Sherlock got his walkie-talkie back. (He told me later that he knew that the men would take it away if they caught us, and he would never see it again.)

"I'll bet they each get twenty years or more," Brandon rejoiced, as Robert prepared to serve one last breakfast. "The police didn't find the money, but the notebook should be enough evidence to put them away for a long time. I just hope they can tie the whole thing in to Senator Greene so he gets his fair share of prison time."

Robert appeared with a huge tray of homemade blueberry waffles, and Maimee followed with several varieties of syrup. "Don't hold your breath waiting for Senator Greene to go to jail," the little caretaker rasped. "It's my guess that he'll slip out of this like a greased eel."

"Not this time," Brandon replied. "The notebook has his handwriting! He slipped up."

Robert shook his head. "Doesn't matter. He'll get out of it."

Mr. Diamond took the plate of waffles and set them on the table. "Lisa, lead us in prayer, would you please?"

That final breakfast was the best of the week. Robert outdid himself. In addition to the scrumptious waffles, he served sausage and bacon, mushroom and Swiss cheese omelets, and raspberry tarts! I ate like a starving grizzly bear, but Sherlock ate twice as much.

"We need to roll out of here by two o'clock this afternoon," Mr. Diamond said as we finished breakfast. "I'd like for each of you to have your stuff packed and in the van before lunch."

"Thanks for inviting us to Diamond Point," Sherlock told him. "We enjoyed ourselves immensely."

The millionaire smiled. "Glad to have you, all of you. Robert and Maimee and I enjoyed your company."

Sherlock stood to his feet. "I need to take the spotlight back to Aysee's Hardware," he said. "Does anyone want to go with me?"

"Why don't we all go?" Lisa suggested. "I want to tell Norm and Max goodbye." Brandon and I decided that we would go too, so the four of us hurried to the garage and got out the scooters for the final trip to Aysee's. It was to be an outing that I would remember for the rest of my life.

"The spotlight did very well," Sherlock told Max, as he set the two million candlepower spotlight on the counter at the hardware store. "I'm returning it in perfect condition. Thanks for renting it to me."

Max took the spotlight from the box and looked it over. "It is in perfect condition," he agreed. He opened the drawer on the cash register and pulled out a five-dollar bill, which he handed to Sherlock. "Here. Ten dollars is too much rent on a twenty-dollar item."

"We agreed on ten dollars," Sherlock protested.

"I know," Max replied. "But five is aplenty." He looked at Sherlock. "So this is yer last day here, huh? Will ya do somethin' fer me? Seein' how it's yer last day and all?"

Sherlock shrugged. "Sure. What is it?"

"Tell us how ya could always tell Norm and me apart." Norm must have been listening to the whole conversation because just then he popped out of the back room and approached the counter. I held my breath. Would Sherlock tell? I noticed that Lisa and Brandon also waited eagerly to see what he would do.

"I'll give you all a hint," Sherlock teased. "You're right-handed and Norm is left-handed. That's how I could tell you apart."

Both men had their hands on the counter at that instant, and I leaned over and studied them closely. But like everything else about them, their hands were identical. "Sherlock," I complained, "that doesn't help a bit. Come on, just tell us!"

"As you may have noticed," Sherlock replied, "both men keep a yellow pencil over their right ear. Max is right-handed and reaches for the pencil with his right hand, so the point always faces forward. Norm reaches for his pencil with his left hand, so the point always faces backwards. It's that simple."

My gaze flew to the pencils, and, of course, Sherlock was right. It *was* that simple! I felt like screaming. Why couldn't we have noticed that?

"Sherlock, you should be a detective," Max said, once we had all recovered from the shocking simplicity of Sherlock's explanation. Sherlock just grinned at him.

As Max engaged Sherlock in conversation, I noticed that Norm slipped away from the counter with a mysterious expression on his face. He motioned for Lisa to follow him to the back of the store. I was dying with curiosity, so I followed at a discreet distance. Lisa and Norm took a seat on a polished old bench beside a display of house paint. I lingered on the next aisle with the ladders so that I could hear. I knew that something was up, but I was totally unprepared for what Norm had to tell Lisa.

"I haven't said anything to Max," Norm began, "but I've been having chest pains this last month or so. Maybe it's nothing, but I've been too afraid to go to the doctor and find out."

Lisa grabbed his arm. "You need to see a doctor right away, Norm. Please?"

The old man nodded. "I will, soon as I git up the courage. But here's what I wanted to ask ya about. Would ya tell me again how to ask God to save me? I don't know how much time I got left, but I ain't about to take any chances."

My eyes filled with tears as Lisa pulled a New Testament from her purse. "You have to admit to God that you're a sinner," she told Norm, leafing through the pages. "Here, look at this Bible verse. 'For all have sinned, and come short of the glory of God.' Do you believe that, Norm? Are you willing to admit to God that you've done wrong?"

The old man nodded. "Up till recently, I've always thought that I was pretty good," he admitted. "Max and I have always been honest and done right by our customers. But I been readin' those little papers ya been givin' us, and I started seein' that I ain't perfect like God."

"The second thing you need to know is that Jesus died for you," Lisa told Norm gently. She showed him the New Testament again. "Look what it says here: 'But God commendeth his love toward us, in that, while we were yet sinners, Christ died for us.' Norm, do you believe that Jesus died for you, and that He rose from the grave after three days?"

To my surprise, Norm began to sob. "Yes, I do," he said softly.

"Then you need to ask Jesus to save you," Lisa said brightly. Listening from the next aisle, I could sense the excitement in her voice. "The tenth chapter of Romans promises: 'For whosoever shall call upon the name of the Lord shall be saved.' Norm, do you want to do that?"

Norm nodded. His chin was quivering. Together, the old man and the young soul-winner bowed their heads in the back of the old hardware store. In a trembling voice, Norm Aysee asked Jesus to be his Savior. I was crying.

Lisa told Brandon and Sherlock about it as we started the motor scooters for the trip back to Diamond Point. Both boys were excited. I thought about what Lisa had done as we sped through the colorful woods. *If Lisa can lead people to the Lord, then can't I do the same? Lord,* I prayed, *help me to learn to lead people to you like Lisa does!* I meant it with all my heart.

When we arrived back at Diamond Point, Robert was checking Mr. Diamond's van for the trip home. We put the scooters in the garage. All four of us headed down to the boathouse and then paddled over to Mrs. Pendergrass's farm to return the canoes and tell her goodbye. "I hate to see you go," the old lady told us, as she gave each of us a brave smile. "I sure enjoyed your company, and I wish you could have come over more often."

"So do we, Mrs. Pendergrass," Brandon said, and I could tell he really meant it.

"I have good news," Lisa announced. "Norm Aysee accepted the Lord as his Savior!"

Mrs. Pendergrass beamed with joy. "Praise the Lord," she rejoiced. "I've been praying for that man for years! When was it?"

"Just a few minutes ago," Lisa replied. "It's an answer to prayer for me too. Now we have to pray for Max."

"We'll do it right now," Mrs. Pendergrass declared. Bowing her head, she thanked God for Norm's salvation, prayed for his brother Max, and asked for a safe trip home for us. She hugged us all, and we said goodbye.

"There's something I've been wondering about," I told Sherlock, as we hiked back to Diamond Point. "Why did the senator's men use flashing lights to signal each other? Why not just use radios or even telephones to set up the details of the drops? Why flashing lights? That seemed so . . . so primitive."

"Think about it, Penny," Sherlock responded. "Radio signals travel for miles and can be intercepted by anyone with a radio on the right frequency. The transmissions can also be recorded and used as evidence in court. Telephones can be tapped, and conversations can be recorded, again providing evidence in a court of law.

"The light signals were the safest option because the Thunderbird is such a secluded lake. Diamond Point and Briarwood are the only residences on the south wing, and on the north wing it's just the Aysee brothers and the Lewis family. Norm and Max go to bed early every night, and the plane always came in fairly late."

I shrugged. "OK, that makes sense."

Mr. Diamond was carrying luggage to the van when we got back. He looked at Sherlock as we approached. "Got some bad news for you, pal. The District Attorney's office just called ten minutes ago. They're not being allowed to pursue the case against Senator Greene and his staff. The notebook was returned to Briarwood this morning, and the entire case is to be dropped."

Sherlock was shocked. "But why?" he protested. "We didn't have a tight case against them, but a thorough investigation was certainly in order. I'm sure that they could have uncovered enough evidence to put them away for a long time."

The millionaire shook his head. "It's not going to happen."

I was angry. "But what about the kidnapping charges against Carl and Lucas and . . ."

"Look on the bright side, Penny," Mr. Diamond said softly. "Senator Greene will have to move his money laundering operation somewhere else, now that a few people are aware of what he's doing. I don't think he'd dare continue business as usual."

"But it's not fair," I stormed. "He's breaking the law!"

"Don't leave here frustrated because it seems that Senator Greene is getting away with his crimes," Mr. Diamond told us.

"He'll answer to God one day." He smiled at me. "And we've had a good time together, haven't we?"

"It has been a good week," I admitted. "We did solve the mystery of the phantom airplane even if we couldn't do much to put the senator out of business. And we had a lot of fun, and caught a few fish, and . . ."

"And saved the life of little Melissa Lewis," Brandon interjected.

"And helped Norm Aysee get saved," Lisa finished.

"Well, let's have lunch and then hit the road, shall we?" Mr. Diamond said. "It's been a good week together."

"Amen," Lisa and I said in unison. "It's been a great week!"